James Kn
3-26-2

ALL APPEALS DENIED

TO: JIM ASHCRAFT,
A GOOD FRIEND FOR 63 YEARS, WHOSE BETTER HALF, LOIS, HAS ALSO BEEN A GOOD FRIEND DURING ALL THOSE YEARS.
BEST WISHES TO YOU & YOURS,

James Knox

Jimmy

* SEE DEDICATION PAGE.

Library of Congress Control Number:
ISBN: 978-1-937183-30-1 Softcover

This is a work of fiction. Names, characters and incidents either are the product of the author's imagination or are used fictitiously, and any resemblance to any actual persons, living or dead, or events is entirely coincidental. In almost every case, the locales are real.

This book was printed in the United States of America.

To order additional copies of this book, please contact:
JWK Books at 1-864-313-0836 (Verizon Cell #) and YOU WILL RECEIVE A SIGNED COPY; or contact A LOCAL BOOKSTORE and give them the correct ISBN number for Hardcover or Softcover shown above on this page. NOTE: Please be sure to furnish the correct ISBN number in order to receive the book you want.

ACKNOWLEDGMENTS

MANY THANKS:

To my wife, Pam, for assisting in many ways to “move this book along to completion”.

To my mother-in-law, Millie Reiberg, for her suggestions and advice (usually requested, but sometimes unrequested). One of her unrequested suggestions played a major role in my adding over 7,500 words, after I thought I had completed the book. Mil also edited the manuscript.

To my father-in-law, Dale Reiberg, who often asks thought-provoking questions, such as: “Jim, how do you think-up all that stuff?”

To my ole’buddy, Paul Davis, who, pound for pound was the most ferocious tackler I ever encountered on a football field (I was always thankful that we were on the same team, and that I was tackled by him only in practice); for encouraging me in many ways.

To Dot Richardson, a dear friend of the Reibergs for over forty-years, and since then, my friend, too; for reading the manuscript and making a few “gentle, but well placed comments” that also played a role in the addition of the 7,500 plus words referred to above.

To Terisa Glover, proprietor of The General Store in downtown Lakeland, for her helpful suggestions relating to punctuation that made the book easier to read. This book, “All Appeals Denied”, along with my first book, “Deadly Revenge”, are available at The General Store, 125 South Kentucky, Lakeland, Fl.

Terisa has books written by forty-three local Authors available in her store. Drop by, you'll enjoy your visit there; it's an interesting store.

And last but not least: To my daughters; Merry, Kyle, Jaime and Patti; just for being my daughters.

DEDICATION

I, James Knox, take pride in dedicating this book to eight of my longtime close friends; whose views on matters written about in this book closely parallel my own. (They are listed in alphabetical order; with the city of their current residence following.)

James (Jim) Ashcraft, Spartanburg, SC
James E. (Jim, or "Judge") Davis, Jr. (1933-2009), Abbeville, SC
Paul Davis, Columbia, SC
C.C. (Charlie) Duff, Greenwood, SC
Coy Helms, Greenville, SC
Frank Jones, Woodruff, SC
Frank ("Dink") Staples, Atlanta, GA
Jim Wrenn, Columbia, SC

PROLOGUE

Capital punishment is a highly controversial subject in the United States; and it is usually imposed by judges only in premeditated murder cases, where the evidence clearly proves that the murder was planned. Sixteen of the United States and Washington, D C do not have the death penalty, and they are: Alaska, Hawaii, Illinois, Iowa, Maine, Massachusetts, Michigan, Minnesota, North Dakota, Rhode Island, Vermont, West Virginia, Wisconsin, New Jersey, New Mexico, New York and Washington, D C.

Capital Punishment is a subject on which everyone has a firm opinion; they either strongly oppose it, or they strongly favor it. Personally, I, James Knox, the writer of this book, "strongly favor" Capital Punishment; you know the kind—not an eye for an eye; rather two-eyes for one-eye. However, everyone has a right to his or her own opinion.

I have put many, many hours into writing "All Appeals Denied"; so naturally, I appreciate your reading it. And if anyone who reads this book feels the urge, or the need, to write one opposing the death penalty I will be happy to read it.

Have a good read. I thank you.

James Knox

CHAPTER ONE

SAMMY PAUL was a black man, kinda' shiny-black; he was an honest man; he was a good man; and he was a hard-working man; he was a man who stood six-feet seven-inches; and even though he weighed only 185 he was sinewy, lean and muscular, with broad, sloping shoulders, and very long arms, with hands so large he could handle a basketball with one hand easier than most men could handle the much smaller soccer-ball. To summarize: Those who knew Sammy real well have been heard make such comments as: "He's a quiet, gentle, unassuming man, with gentlemanly manners and other good qualities; one of which is: he's a God-fearing man".

Sammy would later become self-educated in the vocational-field; although he was barely able to read and write when he reached the age of fourteen. He obtained and read books that educated him in the Trades, including: Electricity, Carpentry, Mechanics and other related vocational trades. Perhaps his strongest asset was the common sense he applied to everyday living.

His parents owned a seventy-seven acre farm, on which Sammy was required to work from sun-up until sun-down, six-days a week. Every Sunday, he could be found sitting between his parents, Booker T. and Pearl Paul, on the left front-row of Shady Grove Church in the Watts community of rural Abbeville County, South Carolina. Abbeville and Calhoun Falls are fifteen-miles apart, with Watts sitting about half-way between.

Completely unbeknownst to anyone in advance, the Christmas Season of 1948 would be a dark, sad one for the Paul Family. On the Sunday before Christmas, Sammy's uncle and aunt from

Ninety Six, South Carolina, nine-miles east of Greenwood, drove over to Abbeville to attend services at Shady Grove Church with the Paul Family, where the children of the church performed in their annual Christmas Program. The Wade family, Arthur, Pearl Paul's brother, his wife, Kitty, and their two daughters, Lessie Mae, 15, and Lilly, 13, always attended the Christmas Program at Shady Grove. On this particular Sunday, Sammy asked to ride from the church to the Paul family home with his uncle, aunt and cousins.

Sammy's parents, Booker T. and Pearl, in their black 1935 Ford 2-door sedan, when leaving the church yard were one-car ahead of the Wades, with whom Sammy was riding. Booker T., or "Book", as his friends called him, had about two thirds of the Paul's car out onto the unpaved road when, over the short but steep hill in the road, came a South Carolina Highway Department work-truck at full-speed, with a state highway trooper in hot-pursuit.

The angular-impact of the truck into the left door of the Paul vehicle literally bent the car into sort of a U-Shape. The trooper was chasing an escaped chain-gang prisoner from the Abbeville County-Farm Prison when the wreck occurred.

Booker T. and Pearl Paul never knew what hit them; the impact of the much heavier work-truck against the side of the Paul's Ford was delivered with such great force that Book and Pearl were slammed over against the left-side of the car, smashing their heads against the grille of the truck. They didn't suffer; their deaths were instantaneous.

Arthur, Kitty and the two Wade daughters stayed with Sammy until two days after the funeral. Arthur and Kitty told Sammy that they would petition the court for legal custody and take him into the Wade home where he would be treated as if he were their own son, and brother of the girls.

Sammy told Arthur and Kitty, who didn't require much convincing, that he didn't want to go back to school. Arthur Wade worked with the local Greenwood Power Company, ten miles west of their Ninety Six home, and considering the fact that Sammy, although only fourteen, was already six-feet four, Arthur told Sammy that he might be able to get him a job with the power company, but that they would have to 'fib' and tell them that he was sixteen.

Sammy objected, telling his uncle Arthur that his father and mother had taught him all his life to, "never tell a lie, son". But back in those days a lot of paperwork was not required; so Arthur told Sammy that he would tell his foreman that he had a nephew who wanted a job, and that he, "thinks Sammy is sixteen, although he looks eighteen". The minimum age for employment by Greenwood Power Company was sixteen.

The following week, Sammy started work with the power company. Several weeks later, during lunch-time, he was sitting in the shade of a large oak with one of his fellow workers who was reading an Audel Hand Book on how to become an electrician. Within the week, Sammy ordered a copy of the Audel Hand Book for himself; And with the help of his two Wade cousins, Lessie Mae and Lilly, he dug right in and was soon reading with minimum help. It became obvious to his uncle Arthur that Sammy had a natural instinct for understanding electricity, and Arthur and his daughters encouraged him to, "keep at it".

After a year with the Greenwood Power Company, one of the fellows Sammy had worked with there left to work with an electrical contractor who was just beginning to do the electrical work on a two-hundred thousand square foot textile mill being built in Ninety Six, and he recommended Sammy to the contractor. On a job that had to be done during the weekend to accommodate the building contractor, Sammy's friend needed a helper, so he asked his boss if he could bring Sammy in to help. The boss, after observing Sammy working on Saturday and Sunday, offered him a full-time job, at a considerably higher rate of pay than he was making with the power company, so Sammy accepted.

Sammy worked with the electrical contractor for three and a half years and saved most of what he earned; and that, coupled with the very tidy-sum that he was sure to bank if or when he decided to sell his seventy-seven acre home-place in Abbeville County, would provide Sammy a very nice nest-egg.

When he was trying to decide whether to sell or not sell his farm in the Watts community, he thought, "what would Daddy do"? He immediately thought of Mr. T. A. Sherard, President of The Bank of Abbeville. The dollar-wise Mr. Sherard had advised Sammy on financial matters since the death of his parents. Sammy's daddy, Booker T. Paul, had banked with Mr. Sherard for years, so when Sammy started thinking that it might be time to sell his farm; like his father before him, he went to Mr. Sherard for advice.

Mr. Sherard reminded Sammy that two very successful cattle farmers owned the property on both sides of and behind his seventy-seven acres; and then, before continuing, Mr. Sherard got up and closed his office door. Mr. Sherard then did something that, for him, was very unusual—he took a seat on the opposite side of his desk from where he usually sat; about three-feet from Sammy.

Mr. Sherard said, "Sammy, now I'm going to tell you why I suggest you sell your farm at auction. As you know, Mr. Scott owns the cattle farm on the east side of your property, and Mr. Dunn owns the cattle farm on the west side. One day about five or six-years ago Mr. Scott's wife went to spend the day with a life-long lady friend; and Mr. Dunn's wife went shopping in Anderson.

“That afternoon, Mr. Scott was in his pasture, sitting on a blanket beside a pond about three-quarters of a mile behind his house, and Mr. Dunn was in his pasture, sitting on a blanket on a hillside about the same distance behind his house. Both men were deer hunters, and often went on hunting trips together; and along with their wives, frequently visited in each other’s home. Both Mr. Scott and Mr. Dunn always carried their deer-hunting rifles with them when they walked their pastures, because it was well known that bobcats and sometimes packs of wild-dogs roamed the pastures in search of young calves; and neither of them wanted to meet-up with bobcats or wild-dogs without having his rifle with him.

“On this particular day, as he often did, Mr. Scott had removed the scope from his rifle and was sitting on a blanket beside his five-acre pond while panning the countryside with his rifle-scope. As Mr. Scott scoped farther and farther out, he had a clear view of a man and a woman on that hillside blanket going at it as if there was no tomorrow. After watching their frenzied finish on the Dunn blanket, Mr. Scott was ready for some action of his own, and in just a few minutes, he was saddled-up and riding hard.

“Meanwhile, Mr. Dunn was sitting on a blanket on his hillside while panning the countryside with his scope. When Mr. Dunn scoped around the Scott pond, he abruptly stopped when through his scope appeared a man that he quickly concluded was not just doing push-ups; he was adding moves that push-ups don’t include, so he quickly focused on the couple that had, within just a few seconds, scrambled the blanket up into a little wrinkled pile, but they kept pounding away on the thick grass until they finished their session with a burst of action that might have given Mr. Dunn an inferiority complex.

“Having had their afternoon delights, Mr. Scott and Mr. Dunn, still using their scopes, zeroed-in on the blankets once more.

Both of the men happened to be looking directly at each other when they looked through their hand-held scopes; and then—they got the shock of their lives when they focused on the women; both of whom still lay naked on the blankets. Each man, with his scope pressed against his eye, was looking directly at, believe it or not, his own wife.

"From that day forward; Mr. Scott and Mr. Dunn have never spoken to each other, and they have never passed up an opportunity to do the other harm, either. Now, Sammy, you can understand why I suggest that you sell your farm at auction; it's because they both have been trying, for around twenty-years, to buy from your father, what is now your farm. Both Mr. Scott and Mr. Dunn would give almost anything to have your farm, Sammy; and that tells me that one of them, with the other pushing him, would end-up paying two or possibly three times, what it's really worth.

"But keep this in mind, Sammy; if you are planning to sell, don't wait until one of the adjoining property owners dies; because if that happens, you will end up getting only market value for it."

"Mr. Sherard, I thank you very much for your advice. You have just convinced me that I should sell the farm as soon as possible."

Six weeks after Sammy sat down with Mr. Sherard, he acted on Mr. Sherard's advice, and had the farm sold at auction on a sunny Saturday morning. Mr. Scott bought the seventy-seven acres, with house, for 2.7 times the appraised value. Four-weeks later, when Sammy went to the Bank of Abbeville to deposit in his savings account the certified-funds that he received as payment, he delivered to Mr. T.A. Sherard a large smoked ham, twenty-five pounds of smoked bacon and twenty-five pounds of sausage.

Sammy, by the age of eighteen, had finally realized that girls could actually be approached; and that they were as interested in boys as boys were interested in girls; and there was a black-beauty twenty-one miles east of Ninety Six, in the community of Silverstreet; and she really got Sammy's attention. As Judge James E. (Jim) Davis, Jr. (1933-2009) would have said, "She made his socks unravel!" Sammy really went after her, and he reeled her in, too.

Sammy and Lula Mae Paul had been married barely a year when baby Ruth Charlene Paul was brought into the world. Both parents were twenty-two years of age at the time.

When Sammy was only twenty, he had three employees working with him in his electrical business. During the next twenty years, his business steadily grew to the point where he had four three-man crews working five and six days a week; with customers in the territory that encompassed all of northwest South Carolina.

CHAPTER TWO

NOTE: EIGHTEEN YEARS LATER; SAMMY & LULA MAE ARE AGE FORTY AND CHARLENE IS EIGHTEEN. THE YEAR IS 1974.

Silverstreet is a small unincorporated community, but when Lula Mae's parents offered to give them forty acres of land about a quarter-mile from their home, on the condition they build their house there, they jumped on it. After completing and moving into their house, Sammy had the contractor build, on the opposite side of a thick stand of assorted trees that stood about eight-hundred feet from their residence, a building from which to operate their electrical business.

Ruth Charlene Paul, by then a pretty eighteen-year old statuesque young woman, was a freshman day-student at Newberry College, about nine-miles east of their home. Charlene often went to her father's office to see if he had left anything on his desk for her to do; such as letters, invoices, quotes, etcetera, and when he had, she did the work and then took the mail to the post office.

On a mid-April evening, Sammy and Lula Mae were sitting in their screened-porch when the lights of a car turning from the highway into their driveway swept rapidly over the three-hundred feet between highway-34 and their house. When the car was about half-way up the driveway to the Paul's house, Sammy could tell that it was a law-enforcement vehicle, and he wondered aloud to Lula Mae why a sheriff's department car would be coming to their house.

When the car-door opened, Sammy immediately recognized Sheriff Bo Chrisley, and he invited the sheriff in, but he asked Sammy if he could speak with him privately. As Sammy went down the steps, Charlene went into the house. After shaking hands, Sheriff Chrisley asked if Charlene was his daughter, and Sammy anxiously said, "yes, but why are you asking"?

Sheriff Chrisley told him that what he was doing right then was the worst part of being sheriff; and then he told Sammy that Charlene was dead. Sammy staggered as if he had been hit on the head with a hammer, and Sheriff Chrisley moved fast to grab Sammy's arm and prevent his falling to the ground.

When Sammy was able to speak, he asked Sheriff Chrisley what happened; and was told that a man from Newberry and a woman from Saluda had been out on a side-road off highway-121 south, the Saluda Highway, looking for a place "to knock-off a quickie", but after spreading a blanket on the leaves, the woman screamed and pointed to a woman lying still in the leaves about twenty-feet away. Needless to say, they jumped back in their car and drove directly to the sheriff's office. Sheriff Chrisley told Sammy that Charlene's body had been taken to the Newberry County Morgue, and that the medical examiner had confirmed that she had been raped, possibly several times, before she was strangled.

Sheriff Chrisley told Sammy that footprints at the site confirmed that there had been two men at the crime scene.

The sheriff suggested that Sammy have his in-laws, Mott and Daisy Gaines, come over before he told his wife what had happened, and if he wished, he, Sheriff Chrisley, would stop at the Gaines' residence and tell them. The sheriff had known and respected Mott and Daisy Gaines for many years, and he knew that they, too, would be devastated to hear what had happened to their granddaughter; their only grandchild. Sammy told the sheriff that he would appreciate his telling Mott and Daisy. The sheriff, with his hand on Sammy's shoulder, again expressed his deepest sympathy to him and Lula Mae.

Before leaving, the sheriff told Sammy that he was sure they would be talking frequently during the coming days and weeks. Sammy, following Sheriff Chrisley's advice, calmed himself as best he could before returning to Lula Mae, and telling her that the sheriff was investigating a break-in that had occurred between Silverstreet and Newberry a week earlier. He detested lying to Lula Mae, but under the circumstances, he wanted her to be able to draw strength from her parents, both of whom were known to be strong believers in the Almighty; and Sheriff Chrisley was just minutes away from witnessing the remarkable depth of the Gaines' faith.

As expected, Mott and Daisy were shocked, and in a state of disbelief to hear about their granddaughter, but when the sheriff suggested they go to Charlene's parents immediately, they quickly steeled themselves; and while standing erect, with heads bowed and hands locked together, the three of them had a short prayer, in which they included Sheriff Chrisley; and then they locked their house and went over to be with and comfort Lula Mae and Sammy.

On the following Sunday afternoon, four-days after Charlene's murder, the church would hold less than half of the crowd that attended her funeral. Five of the attendees were law enforcement, including Sheriff Chrisley and four of his deputies who, in an effort to blend-in with the crowd, all wore suits instead of their work uniforms. They were unable to detect any suspicious-acting men, and concluded that the murderers were probably not in attendance.

As expected, the funeral was as sad as funerals get. Sammy had to practically carry Lula Mae in and out of the church and to the burial plot. Sheriff Chrisley noticed that, ‘mentally’, Sammy was not at the funeral; but instead, was planning what he would do to the murdering, rapist s.o.b.’s, if and when he got his hands on them. The sheriff was thinking that if he were Sammy, that’s what he, too, would have been thinking.

CHAPTER THREE

On Monday, the day after Charlene's funeral, Sammy went out looking for her car. He reasoned that since Charlene had planned to stay in Newberry for a basketball game, she might have gone to the Newberry College Library to study, or to a downtown sandwich shop for something to eat, or to her favorite ice cream parlor at a strip-shopping center on the bypass out on the east side of town.

He went first to the Library parking lot, but her car wasn't there; so from there, he went to the downtown sandwich shop, and again he struck out. When Sammy passed in front of the ice cream parlor in the end building of the By-Pass Strip-Center, he glanced down the row of parking spaces to the end of the building—and abruptly slammed on his brakes. Charlene's car was parked at an angle to the building in the second parking space from the back of the building.

Sammy opened the door of Charlene's car—and it was when he sat down in the driver's seat that he broke-down; the first time he had done so after learning of her brutal, inhumane rape and murder. Sammy sat there and unashamedly cried and sobbed for at least twenty minutes. And when he finally got over his overdue breakdown, he made an out-loud promise to Charlene: "Angel, I promise you that I will hunt-down the scumbags that did that to you, and when I catch them I will make them suffer in ways that they could never have imagined—they will beg me to kill them before I actually do kill them; and I'm certain they will go straight to hell. Your momma and I will love you forever, Angel. Be sure to save a place up there for us."

Having anticipated that he would find her car, Sammy had thrown a tow-hitch in the back of his van so he could take the car to his place of business and go over it very closely in his search for clues. He didn't have any idea what he was looking for, but he would know it if he found it. Sammy parked Charlene's car in the private double-garage attached to the end of his electrical-business building and padlocked the door with a lock for which only he had a key.

Sammy looked between and under the front seats; and then he looked in the glove-box of the dash, and there, he found a note-pad, on which was an apparently hurriedly written note: AGH-729, 2-guys, blue Dodge, Tue. & Wed. When Sammy saw what was written on that note-pad, his heart nearly stopped. He immediately interpreted Charlene's note as: license plate number; two guys in a blue Dodge on Tuesday and Wednesday; and Sammy thought to himself, "Those two bastards had probably been aggravating and harassing her; accounting for the note. Wednesday was the day she died."

During the sixties and seventies, the South Carolina Highway Department published a book that looked very much like a Sears & Roebuck Catalog of that era. It contained the owner's name, address, make of vehicle and the license plate number. The books were furnished to all law enforcement agencies in the state.

To say Sammy was excited would be a huge understatement; he was beside himself. He knew a policeman named Leo who worked the night-shift in Ninety Six; so he immediately headed there. His friend was sitting behind the desk in the tiny police department office when Sammy arrived. He told Leo that he needed to see his vehicle registration book. Leo took the book into the restroom and placed it on a small table in the corner behind the open door. He told Sammy to lock the door while he was in there; and then pointed out that he was not supposed to let anyone see that book. Sammy assured Leo that it would forever remain their secret.

The note that Sammy slid down in his shirt pocket was priceless to him. He felt certain that he had identified a car used by two men who, at the very least, had aroused Charlene's suspicion. Otherwise, why would she have written the note Sammy found in her car? The name he had taken from the vehicle registration book was: Willie Artavious Spencer, 595 Sunflower Lane, Saluda, SC. Sammy drove directly to Saluda from Ninety Six.

Out on the edge of Saluda, Sammy found a phone booth beside a service station. He called the station, which was less than a hundred feet from the phone booth, and asked for directions from the downtown square to Sunflower Lane. After receiving the directions, with the receiver still up to his ear, Sammy stayed in the phone booth for a couple of minutes after watching the man in the station hang up his phone. He didn't want the man to know that he was the one making that call; so he didn't even look in that direction after ending the call.

By following the man's accurate directions, Sammy ended up directly in front of 595 Sunflower Lane; a rural street off Hwy-121, a mile outside the Saluda City Limits; which accounted for the absence of street lights on the unpaved dead-end street. But when turning around in the tiny cul-de-sac at the end of the street, Sammy's lights landed on a blue Dodge parked about thirty-feet from the street, providing him with a clear view of the license plate he was looking for—South Carolina, AGH-729. The sight of the car and it's license plate caused Sammy's emotions to overcome him, and tears flowed freely down his face as he drove back to the highway; while fighting all the way the urge to rush up to the front-door of 595 Sunflower Lane, and with his riot shotgun in hand, kick down the front door and kill anything that moved on the inside of that house. But the farther he got from that blue Dodge, the clearer his thinking became.

At six o'clock the next morning, Sammy parked at an old run-down closed-down service station building about two hundred yards past the turn-off from Hwy-121 onto Sunflower Lane. He was determined to see where the 1961 Dodge went, and even more importantly, who was in that car.

When it was about a hundred-yards from the highway, Sammy saw the Dodge coming out Sunflower Lane; so he cranked his green work-van and prepared to roll-out. The driver of the Dodge barely slowed-down at the stop sign, much-less stop. He could see three heads in the car as it turned left and headed toward Saluda. Sammy eased onto the road, and gradually closed the gap between his van and the Dodge. When they reached the middle of downtown Saluda, Sammy was next in-line behind the Dodge, but was doing nothing to indicate that he even saw the Dodge. He followed it through town and stayed far enough behind to not arouse suspicion as they continued out Highway-121 north toward Newberry.

As they approached Newberry, the Dodge stayed on highway-121 as it looped north around the city, taking traffic past the numerous industrial plants located along that road. When they reached a box manufacturing plant on the left, the Dodge turned in, but Sammy pulled over into the yard of a convenience store on the opposite side of the road. Being only a hundred or so yards from where the Dodge stopped for a man to get out of the back seat, Sammy estimated him to be middle-aged. The Dodge came down the drive from the box factory and turned left, the same direction they had been going before stopping to let the man out at the plant; probably his workplace.

CHAPTER FOUR

Sammy followed them as they drove southeast, and then it dawned on him; they were headed directly toward where he had found Charlene's car just the day before. That thought started his heart pumping faster. He reached over and placed his hand on his 12-gauge riot shotgun that held ten rounds of buckshot, including the round in the chamber—and that made him feel better, and safer, too.

The Dodge turned in at the strip-shopping center and parked at the end of the strip-center, right up against the side wall of the ice cream parlor that Charlene liked so well. Sammy parked in front of the ice cream parlor, got out of his van and hurried the few steps to the corner of the building; and peeped around to see what the fellows in the Dodge were doing. They had stopped two parking spaces past where Sammy had found Charlene's car; and the Bro' that wasn't driving was out of the car, looking intently for something all-around where her car had been parked; and then he said to the Bro' still in the car, "I don't see nuthin' nowhere out heah!"

He jumped back in the car, and while Sammy, not wanting to be seen, hurried into the restaurant beside the not-yet-open ice cream parlor; the driver backed the Dodge toward the front of the building, parked in the fourth space from the front of the building, leaving just two spaces between the Dodge and Sammy's van. They went into the restaurant and took seats at the counter that's placed parallel to the back wall of the building. That had them facing the back of the restaurant from about ten-feet away.

Sitting unnoticed in a hi-back booth, about ten-feet forward of where the Bros' were being served from behind the counter by a Sista, was Sammy Paul. With Sammy facing the front of the restaurant and the Bros facing the back, they didn't see him, which was the way he wanted it.

The Sista' behind the counter, mistakenly thinking she was keeping her gleeful voice low enough to not be heard, said to the Bros', "How'd y'all make-out wid'da Sista' dat tole'y'all to 'git-lost' last Wednesday?" One of the Bros' said, "Oh we made out real-good wid' huh, real-good! Didn'we, Bro'?" The other Bro' said, "Man yeah', we both got'er—we made'a blieva' outa' huh, sho'did, Sista'. She won't be'tellin' no'body else'ta 'git lost', an'ya can bet'on'nat!"

Sammy could take no more—he left the booth and rushed to his van, jerked the passenger side door open, which couldn't be seen from the restaurant, threw the towel aside and grabbed his riot-shotgun; and after taking three steps toward the restaurant, he suddenly remembered lying awake in bed the night before and planning what he would do to the murdering-rapists of his and Lula Mae's precious-daughter when he got his hands on them; so he was able to get a grip on himself, and put the shotgun back in place and cover it with the towel.

Sammy then got in his van and drove across the parking lot, where those who had seen him would think he had left the area. But after cutting around the block, he went in from another direction and parked in the same place he had just left. His work-van was equipped to haul what, in the electrical field, was considered heavy equipment, such as: sophisticated electrical control panels; large electrical disconnect boxes; magnetic starters and other items that had to be secured in-place in order to prevent damage in transit; and all that required having an independent structure fabricated and installed in the back of the van that would withstand the tremendous securing-forces of, among other things: cables, chains, load binders, turn-buckles and come-a-longs that would be used to secure whatever he needed to put back there. And today he planned to put two sorry-ass s.o.b.'s back there—for what just might be their last ride.

Between the two front seats and the load securing structure in back was a divider made of half-inch diameter steel rods with three-inch square openings, all of which were welded at every rod crossing-point, after which, the divider was welded in-place. The only doors accessing the load-area of the van were the glassless, reinforced double-doors in the back-end, with a hardened hasp and a hardened padlock. Some people thought Sammy must have had his van retrofitted to Fort Knox Specifications.

Sammy, following Sheriff Chrisley's necessary visit to deliver the horrible news of Charlene's death, had spent most of his time anticipating what he was going to do when he got his hands on the two murdering rapists that took Charlene's life and ruined his and Lula Mae's lives. And what he had decided to do sent him shopping in Columbia on Saturday; shopping at a store that would have everything he would need. Sammy went to CCSS (Capital City Security Supplies), where he decided on, and bought: handcuffs, leg-irons, shackles, brass-knuckles and two cattle-prods with an extra box of batteries. When he had paid for everything, and had all of it on a hand-truck, and headed for the door, the salesman said, "Sir, I forgot to show you one item that you might want to consider; but go ahead with what you have there, and when you come back in I'll show you The Persuader; I'll be getting it out."

When Sammy brought the hand-truck back inside, the salesman asked him to come into a small side-room, where he had a ten-inch square by five-inch deep box sitting on a table, and the box had only two words printed boldly on it: "THE PERSUADER".

When Sammy didn't immediately realize what 'the persuader' was used for, the salesman reached in the box, whipped-out the instruction sheet, unfolded it and spread it on the table; after which he didn't need to say another word about what it was used for; the picture of a man wearing one explained everything crystal-clear.

The elasticized belt would fit around the waist of the man, and the three "small-linked" chains attached on one-end to the belt—were attached on the other-end to a soft, pliable, fabric-type copper material woven of hair-size copper threads, with a narrow elastic strip attached on each side to provide a snug fit on the man's 'jewel-bag'. The 115-volt single phase AC power supply was variable by means of an in-line transformer between the electrical outlet and the copper bag. Just looking at the picture of a man wearing that outfit could be enough to cause him to tell the person with the transformer-control anything he wanted to know; and possibly some stuff he would rather not have heard.

After viewing the photo and reading the instructions, Sammy looked the salesman in the eyes, and with a faint smile drawing back the corners of his mouth, said, "I'll take two'a these."

The astonished salesman said, "Two?" While still looking the salesman in the eyes, Sammy said, "Yes, two." Then the surprised salesman said, "Mister, I'd sure hate to be on your 'to-do-list'!" Then Sammy said, "That tells me that you're a very smart man, sir."

What Sammy had heard the two Bros' and the Sista' in the restaurant saying about someone—someone who, without a doubt was Charlene—would soon bring down upon those two dumb-asses a special kind of hell that they couldn't possibly have envisioned. If the punks had had a clue as to the pain and suffering Sammy Paul would inflict upon them during the next twenty-four hours, they might have chosen instead, to go out to Interstate-26 and step out in front of a fast moving big-rig, in which case death would have come instantly; instead of over a period of many hours that would seem more like years to those two cocky, murdering bastards.

CHAPTER FIVE

Sammy looked around the strip-center parking area for the Dodge, and finally found it parked on the end of the lot, right up against the side of the ice cream parlor, only three-spaces from where his van was parked.

In the back of his van, Sammy had a two-foot by three-foot by eight-foot wooden box, and it was full of heavy electrical equipment and parts. The weight stenciled on the box was 688 lbs., so obviously Sammy needed help to unload that box into a building he owned over in Greenwood County, between Chappells and Ninety Six. He positioned himself on the northwest side of the building, about a foot back from the front-corner of the ice cream parlor, but still close enough to the front to be able to hear the two big-mouth Bros well before they reached the corner, where Sammy waited.

Sammy reasoned that those two arrogant, ignorant, big-mouth bastards couldn't possibly keep their damned mouths shut long enough to walk quietly from the restaurant to the corner of the building. When Sammy heard them they were about half-way across the front of the ice cream parlor; and headed toward where he waited around the corner for the right moment to make his move. Just seconds later, Sammy turned the corner and walked rapidly toward them; and then, faking surprise at seeing them, he stopped suddenly and said, "Hey—would you fellows like to make twenty-dollars each for riding out toward Ninety Six and helping me unload a box into a building? We could be back here in less than an hour."

They were so excited to hear that someone would pay them twenty-bucks each for an hour of work, while most of the time sitting on their asses, they couldn't hide their excitement, and one of them blurted out, "Bro, fu' twenty dollars a'piece we'd consida' killin' somebody. Man yeah, we'll do'it, where's yo' ride?" Sammy pointed toward his van, and they eagerly headed that way.

When Sammy swung one of the van's back doors open the Bros jumped right in and seated themselves on the box they were going to help unload. Sammy closed the door behind them and padlocked it. He took highway-121 toward Saluda and five miles out, forked right on highway-34, toward Silverstreet, Ninety Six and Greenwood. Midway between Chappells and Ninety Six, Sammy turned left onto a private road. After unlocking, driving thru and relocking the gate, he drove the half-mile to the building that, years earlier, was The Chappells Abattoir, a beef and pork processing facility that had served upstate South Carolina for many years, before closing about fifteen-years earlier.

Seven years earlier, Sammy had bought a hundred and sixty-nine acres of land, with building, at an auction conducted by Hilton L. Dodgen & Sons Auction and Realty of Greenwood, SC. It was sold at public auction to settle an estate. He bought it for the land only, but a close inspection of the building revealed that all it needed was a new roof, (two) new heavy-duty rollup doors, and some serious cleaning and painting. Sammy had a building contractor from Greenwood do the roof and doors, while he and two of his employees did the cleaning and painting.

From its days as an abattoir building, crossbars, hangers, hooks, overhead conveyors and other slaughter-house equipment remained in place in the building.

Sammy backed up to the front roll-up door, went inside, raised the door, backed the van inside, lowered the door, took out his riot shotgun, and then removed the items he had bought at Capital City Security Supplies and spread them on a bench along the side-wall and then unlocked the handcuffs and shackles. With his riot shotgun in one hand and two handcuffs in the other, Sammy returned to the cab of his van. After standing his shotgun up against the dash, he turned to face the Bros, each of whom, by then, had a very concerned expression on his face.

Sammy said, "Where were you two last Wednesday evenin'?!" The Bros looked at each other, then, as if joined at the hip, they turned and lunged against the back doors of the van, but bounced back. Then realizing that they were now the prisoners of a highly motivated, dangerously pissed-off, physically capable man, they looked at each other, but still said nothing, not a word. Sammy grabbed his riot shotgun and rapidly racked a round into the chamber, scaring the crap out of both of them. While giving them the meanest stare he could conjure-up, Sammy yelled, "I said where wuz' y'all last Wednesday evenin'?! Again they looked at each other, but said nothing, still not a word.

Sammy got out and walked around to the rear of the van and unlocked the padlock, but left it hanging in the hasp; then he went over to the table and picked up two handcuffs before returning to the cab. He snapped one 'cuff' around a half-inch rod of the divider-grille separating the cab from the cargo area, and then pushed the matching cuff thru a three-inch opening of the divider-grille to the Bro nearest the grille, and said, "Snap this cuff around your right wrist—and hurry-up!" When Sammy raised his voice, the Bro again nearly crapped in his britches, but immediately snapped the cuff around his wrist. By then the eyes of both were very near the size of silver-dollars!

Sammy had become irritated and it was reflected in his speech. He then shoved the other handcuff thru to the other Bro and said, "Put this on your right wrist and snap it shut, and do it now!" It was done in a flash, and Sammy said to him, "I'm comin'roun' to th'back'o th'van an'open th'door, an'if ya'try anything I'll blo'yo damn head'off! Do'ya unda'stan?!" "Yes'suh, I'heah you; I ain't gonna' try nuthin'." With the handcuff around his right wrist, he moved to the back of the van, just as he had been told to do. Sammy removed the padlock from the hasp and placed it on the van's bumper.

Before letting the Bros out of the van, Sammy told them that he didn't want to know their names, but that so they would know which one of them he was talking to, he was going to call them number-one and number-two, and that the one he let out first would be number-one.

When Sammy opened the door, number-one, the unrestrained Bro, sprang out directly toward him, but Sammy was anticipating his move, and with his shotgun gripped firmly in his huge hands, he introduced number-one to Mr. Gun-Stock Butt-Plate on the back-end of his riot shotgun. The stock butt-plate smashed squarely across his forehead, sending him sprawling onto the concrete floor; knocked-out cold as a cucumber; and sporting the clear imprint of the gun-stock butt-plate just above his eyebrows.

Sammy dragged him over to a chain-hoist hanging from an overhead monorail, snapped the already-open cuff around his left wrist, stepped over to an electrical disconnect box on the wall and pushed the lever up to the on position, powering-up the hoist, and then he lowered the hook of the hoist nearly to the floor and hooked it under the handcuffs between the still-out-cold number-one, and with the hoist, lifted him straight-up—until his feet dangled a foot above the floor.

Sammy, with his shotgun gripped tightly in his hands, stepped up to the back of the van and said to number-two, "Do'ya think'ya can do'as I tell'ya, or should'I jus'go on an'put th'butt-plate'uv this gun across your head now?" With the fear of God and Sammy showing clearly on his face, number-two said, "Nawsuh, I ain't gonna' give'ya no trouble." Sammy told him, "We'll try to do'it without me hittin'ya or shootin'ya—but if'ya try anything, you'll get what he got, or worse. Now I'm comin' aroun'ta th'front and unlock that han'cuff, but I'm gonna'lock this door first."

Sammy climbed into the cab and unlocked number-two's handcuff, then returned to the back door, and cautiously opened it, and while stepping backwards he raised his shotgun to his shoulder. The Bro said, "Don't shoot! I ain't gonna'do nuthin, mistah!, I swear I ain't!" Sammy said, "If you do it'll be th'last move you evva'make. Now lock that cuff aroun' your otha' arm, and hurry up!"

Sammy noticed number-one regaining consciousness, so he ordered number-two to remove number-one's clothes, and handed him a closed knife with which to cut his clothes off. He told number-two to open the knife slowly, and to not even think about making a move toward him; and then without warning, and just for effect, Sammy fired a load of buckshot into the side of a large cardboard box of rags sitting about five-feet from number-one, causing number one to do number-two; when number-one got a look at what that load of buckshot did to that box, his eyes returned to silver-dollar size, or maybe bigger.

With Sammy holding his riot-shotgun on him, number-two, using Sammy's knife, completely cut-up and stripped away every stitch of clothing number-one had been wearing. And then, Sammy told number-two to close the knife and lay it on the table, and when he had done that, he told the two of them to swap places; after which number-one, then naked as a jaybird, cut and stripped the clothes from number-two, after which number-one, the one with the badly swollen forehead, was ordered to pull another chain-hoist over to within twenty-feet of number-two.

The number-two Bro suddenly yelled, “Mista, why don’tcha juss go on and givvus’a whuppin and take’us back tu’town. It’s gettin’late an’I gotta’ six o’clock date—an’I don’t wanna’ be late! Whut’s du’matta wid’you, man?” Sammy was furious; and he ran over to number-two and pushed a cattle-prod up between his legs, pressed the button, and held it up in there for about thirty-seconds; and if number-two’s screams were not heard all the way up to the half-mile away highway, it was because no one was there to hear them.

Sammy told number-two to raise his hands straight-up above his head, and when he had done so, Sammy moved the chain-hoist over until it was directly above the head of number-two. Using the hand-held push-button control, Sammy raised the chain-hook up to the handcuffs, and told number-two to drop the cuffs connecting-chain over the hoist chain-hook. When the hook had grabbed the chain connecting the cuffs to each other, Sammy started raising the hook until the feet of number-two were about a foot above the floor. He started complaining that the cuffs were cutting into his wrists and Sammy said, “Good!” Shortly after number-two complained of the cuffs cutting into his wrists, number-one made the same complaint, and again Sammy said, “Good!”

In the concrete floor, directly underneath and in-line with the overhead conveyor, from which the punks were hanging, was a row of floor-embedded eye-bolts spaced two-feet apart for a distance of forty-feet. The eye-bolts had been used to hold hogs and cattle taut while they were being processed. It was done by simply hooking the curl on the end of a spring into the eye-bolt and the curl on the opposite end of the spring into the pork or beef; holding it nearly-still while the cutting and trimming was being done.

Sammy locked handcuffs around the ankles of both men; then attached chains to the handcuffs and hooked links of the chains into eye-bolts that were far enough apart to spread their legs as far apart as they could possibly be spread, causing them to start yelling and screaming, but to no avail. They were almost a half-mile from highway-34, the road closest to where they were, and Sammy had locked the gate in the five-strand barbed-wire fence when they came in. Additionally, Sammy had so many "No Trespassing" signs around the perimeter of his 169-acres that it was a much-talked about subject among people in the vicinity of the property. The possibility that someone was going to hear the yells and screams of the thugs was very remote, and Sammy knew that better than anyone.

CHAPTER SIX

Sammy stood about ten-feet out in front of the two Bros as he told them why they were there, as if they hadn't already figured that out. He told them that they had taken the life of the most precious person he and his wife could ever hope to have in their lives. He told them that Charlene's mother, his wife, was crying about twenty-hours a day, and not just because she was taken from them, but also because of the way she was taken; how she had suffered, how she had been humiliated, how she had been embarrassed, how she would never be able to attain her goals, and then Sammy had to stop talking because he was choking-up.

When he was able to continue, he told them that it was now time for them to pay the price for what they had done. And then he told them that they were going to die—and die that day; but that death would not come quickly to them. He told them that if he could kill them fifty times, that still would not be enough for them to pay. He told them that he had never thought he would be able to enjoy killing someone—but that in this case he was going to make an exception, that he had an overwhelming, burning desire to kill them. He told them that he heard what they said about Charlene in the restaurant that morning, and when they started to say they didn't really mean what they said, he told them they were damned liars, and to shut up!, or he'd ram a cattle-prod up their rear-ends.

Sammy walked over to the table and picked up one of the boxes that had two words on the front: "The Persuader". He opened the box and took out the picture of a man sporting "The Persuader". While wearing rubber gloves, Sammy walked up to number-two, and told him he could be first. When they finally figured out what the persuader was, they both lost control—and pissed all over the floor.

With his rubber gloves on, Sammy installed a persuader on number-one while he screamed, yelled, hollered, and then finished clearing his bladder; and when Sammy started toward number-two, he let everything fly, the least of which was the clearing of his bladder. After the persuaders were installed, Sammy plugged them into two nearby receptacles, but instead of starting with low voltage and building-up gradually, as the instructions suggested, he instantly dialed them up to maximum voltage, and for a few minutes it seemed that both punks would surely pass-out.

They screamed, hollered, yelled, cursed, and then seemed to get a sudden-case of religion, as they talked quite a lot to God—and then they started begging forgiveness and mercy from Sammy; but Sammy yelled back to them, "I can't hear you!!" When they started sweating profusely, Sammy started rapidly running the voltage up and down, up and down, and that did cause them to beg and plead; to which Sammy yelled, "I still can't hear you!!"

Sweat was pouring off them; causing them to look as if they were standing under a yard sprinkler. And then, images of what those scumbags did to his and Lula Mae's daughter started flashing before his eyes; rendering him incapable of having one iota of mercy for the two cowardly assholes that he considered scum of the earth.

With the horrible, despicable crimes those two sub-human murdering, gutless punks inflicted upon his daughter fresh in his mind, Sammy described the plan he had for the two of them: He told them that the two eight-foot square, two-foot deep vats that were mounted on casters, and sitting behind where they were already hanging by their arms, would be used to catch their blood, instead of having it spill all over the clean floor. At that time, number-two, the most cocky and arrogant of the two murderers, said, “You jus’jokin’bout’dat blood aint’cha, Bro?” Sammy, after staring at him for thirty-seconds or longer, said, “Don’t’cha call me Bro, you sorry, worthless sonofabitch, and hell’no I’ain’t jokin’bout’da blood—yo’blood, ya’bastard!”

Sammy opened the driver side-door of his van and pulled a ten-inch blade, razor-sharp hunting knife from a scabbard that was snapped to the front of the seat. When he walked back behind the van, number-one and number-two started yapping at the same time; both of them were jabbering so incoherently that all he could make of what they were saying was, “Man, whut’cha gonna’do wid’dat knife?” To which Sammy replied, “You’ll find out soon’enuff.”

Sammy took a bag from the cab of his van and went into a small office in the front corner of the building. When he came out, over his clothes he was wearing plastic coveralls that completely covered his body from his neck to his feet, and he was wearing rubber boots instead of his street shoes, and the boots came almost up to his knees, and they were inside the legs of his pants. When he put on the clear plastic shield that dropped over his head and came down to his shoulders, he was totally protected from the blood that would soon be spewing from the two worthless thugs.

To make his job easier, Sammy placed ether saturated towels over the faces of both thugs, and when they were finally convinced that he really was going to relieve them of their privates, they begged him to put them to sleep. Sammy rolled the vats forward, placing one underneath each of the murdering rapists. And he then further saturated the towels with ether. He told them to lay their heads back so they would be looking straight up at the ceiling. When they had assumed the position, Sammy walked over to each of them and placed a towel over his face.

When the bodies of both murderers 'went limp', Sammy, still wearing his rubber gloves, stepped up to number-two and quickly relieved him of what he should have kept in his pants the previous Wednesday. He then placed 'the harvest' on the ether-soaked towel still resting on the face of number-two. After that he stepped across to number-one and repeated the procedure on him.

Sammy then moved over to number-one and removed the towel on which lay a useless assemblage of body parts. He held the murderer's mouth open and deftly transplanted the parts, still encased in their natural, lifelong container. He pushed a 'nearly-round part' into each jaw-cavity, with them still in their natural container, and that left only the 'shriveled appurtenance' hanging out through the center of his lips—resting meekly on his chin.

Sammy, like all good surgeons, wanted his work to be as neat as possible; so he went to the van and lifted from his tool-box, a heavy-duty hand-held electric stapling machine, capable of stapling large, thick, Gaylord corrugated boxes; and after making sure everything was properly placed, he took the punk's lips between his gloved-fingers and pulled them out far enough to get one of his heavy-duty staples over and through the thick, double lips on each side of the 'appurtenance', leaving it perfectly centered between each side of his mouth.

Sammy then moved back over to number-two and repeated the procedure that already graced the face of number-one. After standing there admiring his handiwork for a couple of minutes, he went to his van, brought out his Polaroid Camera, and proceeded to take a dozen pictures of the two murdering s.o.b.'s who should have danced-all-night, instead of spending their afternoon raping and murdering an innocent young woman.

Sammy would now drive over to Greenwood and tell his attorney what he had done, and face the music; he even had visions of the court ruling ‘justifiable homicide’.

After moving the van outside and locking the doors, he reloaded the towels with more ether and placed them back on the Bros’ faces.

After stepping out the front door, Sammy hesitated there about ten seconds, then stepped back inside, walked over to within fifteen-feet of the dead bastards, looked back and forth from one punk to the other several times, and then yelled as loud as he could:

“You lousy sons-of-bitches!!!, may you rot in the deepest pits of hell!!!” That seemed to calm Sammy, and he immediately felt much better.

CHAPTER SEVEN

Sammy stopped at the Panorama Lodge, just a couple of miles west of the abattoir, toward Ninety Six, and called his attorney's office. His secretary told Sammy that Mr. Wham was with a client, but that she would have him return the call. Sammy told her that he was on his way to their office, and should be there within thirty minutes. He thanked her, and proceeded toward Greenwood.

When Sammy reached the second of only two traffic lights in Ninety Six, it was green, but just as he was passing underneath the light, a long, dark-blue Fleetwood Cadillac, headed south and driven by a ninety-four year old lady, at what the eye-witness policeman estimated to be fifty-five to sixty miles per hour in a fifteen-mile per hour zone, smashed into the right-hand side of Sammy's work-van. The impact threw him over against the right side of the cab and knocked him out-cold. He was rushed eight-miles to Self Memorial Hospital on the south side of Greenwood; where it was soon determined that he was comatose.

The ninety-four year old woman driving the Cadillac, according to the policeman, was referred to throughout Greenwood County and beyond, as "Ms. Money-Bags". Fortunately, she was wearing her seat belt, and didn't get a scratch on her, even though she was said to be "falling-down-drunk" when she smashed into Sammy's van. It was common knowledge all over Greenwood County that she had had dozens of wrecks, and caused many others, over the years; all her fault, for which she received traffic tickets that somehow managed to "conveniently get lost in the mail" somewhere between Greenwood and the state highway department in Columbia, the state capitol, just sixty-five miles away. The fact that her driver's license had never been suspended was public knowledge. The public also knew that she was filthy-rich, which meant she had political-pull, which meant she was not likely to lose her license—at least not before she kills someone.

A week had passed and Sammy was still comatose; and people were wondering out loud, "Why are buzzards circling over the old abattoir out near Chappells? Has somebody cranked it back up?" In Ninety Six, so many people were talking about the buzzards that Greenwood County Sheriff Doolittle was called, and he promptly dispatched a couple of deputies out there to check it out.

He sent a male deputy and a female deputy, and when they reached the gate at the driveway into the old abattoir, they removed the lock that Sammy had placed back through the hasp, but unlike him, had failed to snap it into locked position. The deputies decided to put Sammy's lock in their car and use one of the locks carried in all the sheriff's department cars, for which every deputy in the department had a master-key. The sheriff's lock-policy had often proved to be a good one.

About half way from the highway to the abattoir building, the deputies spotted, off to their left, a huge maple tree with long, low-hanging limbs. The two deputies, Brenda Hur and Leo Horne, who had been eyeing each other for several months, started discussing that this late-spring day, with a nice, cool breeze rustling through the leaves and the temperature hanging in the mid-seventies would be the ideal time to spread a blanket under that maple; after all, they were protected by the best Yale lock that money could buy, and they had been waiting months for just such an opportunity—so they quickly decided, "this is the time to do it". And besides that, they reasoned that their car, sitting way-back under those low-hanging limbs, was not likely to be seen, even if someone did succeed in getting past their lock, and drive down that road.

The big maple stood about a hundred-yards off to the left of the private road running from Hwy-34 down to the old abattoir building; so Leo drove the car all the way up to the back side of the maple tree, and then spread the blanket on the grass about fifteen-feet from the tree. Brenda must have been anxious; she started stripping before Leo could unbuckle the tons of equipment deputies and policemen carry around their waist; so Brenda started helping Leo take off his equipment, and his clothes.

With the help of Brenda, who had already stripped buck-naked, Leo was nearly ready for action when he looked over his shoulder and caught Brenda gyrating, bumping and grinding. With a devilish grin on her face, she said, “If you don’t hurry-up, I’m gonna’ start without’cha.” Leo said, “If you promise you’ll do that, I’ll just sit in the car and watch’ya; but I expect’ya to put on hell’uva show.”

Brenda dropped her knees down onto the blanket, placed her hands, with fingers interlocked, behind her head, and pretending that Leo was lying underneath her on his back—she performed what Leo later told her was the greatest dry-run he’d ever seen; and after she’d been at it for three or four minutes, Leo jumped out of the car fully ready for immediate-action, and as soon as Leo was on his back, Brenda climbed on and demonstrated to Leo just what he had been missing, “by not making this happen many months ago”.

While Brenda and Leo were totally oblivious to the world around them, another sheriff’s department car had quietly eased onto the premises and parked with their car facing the blanket-party at a forty-five degree angle. Every single thing that happened on that blanket, including vocal expressions and wild physical activity at crucial moments, was all recorded on the movie-camera the senior-deputy kept in his patrol car.

Now for the rest of the story: With the movie-camera that he kept in the trunk of his car, Deputy Ben Hur, Deputy Brenda Hur's husband, recorded what, at that moment, was maybe the greatest show on earth. Deputy Ben Hur's patrol car left the scene without Leo and Brenda knowing anyone had witnessed them having their afternoon-delight on the blanket; and she would not be made privy to viewing her academy award performance until she was later ordered to do so by the judge in divorce court.

The loving deputies, after first taking care of business, finally got around to doing what the sheriff sent them out there to do. Although the deputies couldn't get into the building, their noses told them that there was death in or around the building. They radioed the sheriff's office, and speaking directly with sheriff Doolittle, told him of their suspicions. The sheriff asked Leo if deputies Hur and Logan had been there; that they had been to Columbia to deliver a prisoner to the state penitentiary, and had called in to report that the prisoner had been delivered, and they were headed back to Greenwood. But after thinking about the situation for a few minutes, the sheriff had called back and told Hur and Logan to stop by the abattoir and ask if they were needed there. They told the sheriff that they would go directly there.

The sheriff told Leo that he was personally coming to the site and to have the gate open. The sheriff called a Greenwood locksmith and asked that he meet him at the old abattoir between Ninety Six and Chappells. The locksmith told sheriff Doolittle that he knew exactly where it was; that he had done some lock-work out there about six or seven years back. Sheriff Doolittle called longtime friend Hilton Dodgen and asked him if he and son Daryl would like to ride out to the old abattoir with him, that two of his deputies said the smell of death was heavy in the air out there. Sheriff Doolittle told Hilton to sit tight; he would pick them up in fifteen minutes.

When the sheriff, accompanied by Hilton and Daryl Dodgen, arrived at the building the locksmith was already there, meaning that there were five men and one woman on site—and they all agreed that there was definitely a heavy-smell of death in the air. Leo told them that he and Brenda had walked a hundred-fifty yards away from the building, in four directions, and that the smell of death grew weaker and weaker as they walked away, but grew stronger and stronger as they walked back toward the building.

The sheriff said that was good enough for him, and gave the locksmith the go-ahead to open it up. In less than ten minutes the door was flung open, but no one rushed in. Finally the sheriff cautiously entered the building, and in less than a minute he ran back out—holding a handkerchief over his nose and mouth while fighting-back the urge to throw-up.

When the sheriff had aired-out his lungs and gathered his wits, he turned toward the other five, and while looking directly at her, said, “Brenda, I don’t want to embarrass you, so if you wish, you may be excused from listening to this; it’s graphic, really graphic.” Brenda replied, “Sheriff, when I accepted this job, I agreed to never ask for or accept special favors; and although I appreciate your consideration, I’ll listen to what you say—like a man, and I’ll be grateful if you don’t sugarcoat what you say.” He said, “I thank you for that, Brenda; you really know how to make it easy on a man.” Leo, facing Brenda from six-feet away, was grinning like a possum when Sheriff Doolittle said to her, “Brenda, you really know how to make it easy on a man”, and the wide-grin on Leo’s face caused Brenda to blush a distinct red.

Sheriff Doolittle said, “Now that Brenda has volunteered to be a man, I’ll try to pretend she is a man, but to do that, I’ll have to not look at her—for obvious reasons. Now, I’ll tell you what I saw inside the building, but to really believe what I tell you I saw, I’m sure you’ll have to see it for yourself, so after I tell’ya, I’ll show'ya. For someone, or ones, to do what has been done to those two in there, he or they, would have had to be highly pissed; just downright mad as hell! If one man did this, he would have had to plan it in detail; and I mean very fine detail, too.

"What's been done in there is this: Both of them are stripped buck-naked, handcuffed, hung-up by their arms on a hoist hook, legs pulled as far apart as they'll go and handcuffed to eye bolts imbedded in the floor; towels drenched in ether placed over their faces to put'em under, and now get ready for this; their privates were cut off, and I mean the whole package was cut clean-off, with what must have been a razor-sharp knife; and this is the most unbelievable part of the whole scene: their full package of privates are crammed in their mouths with everything still in th'bag—one uh, uh, testicle, is in each cheek—excuse me, Brenda, but I warned you that this was gonna'be graphic; and then with his limber-member hanging out through his lips and resting on his chin, his lips were jammed-up against each side of the appurtenance, and now get this—their lips are stapled together on each side of the appurtenance! The man, or men, who killed these ole'boys was mad as hell; they must have done somethin' mighty damn bad to him or a loved one.

"Now, what I really don't understand is why someone would do such a thorough job of killing these ole' boys; but then leave the bodies and a ton of incriminating evidence scattered all over the place. Brenda, please call our office and have one of the ladies go over to the courthouse and find out who owns the old abattoir property. When we get the owner's name, it probably won't take long to find out who killed'em, and why. There is one thing I think all of us can agree on, though; whoever did it was motivated; these ole'boys musta' shore'nuff pissed'off somebody!"

CHAPTER EIGHT

When Sheriff Doolittle was finally standing alone, Hilton and Daryl Dodgen approached him, and Hilton, after glancing back over each shoulder to be sure no one was coming their way, especially the killer, said, "Gordon, Daryl and I sold this property at public auction about seven or eight years ago, so if your people have a problem finding what you need at the courthouse, we can dig-up the name of who bought it at the auction. But as you know, the buyer at the auction might not presently own it—just let me know if you need our help."

"Thank you, Hilton, that's good to know; I'll keep that in mind."

When Sheriff Doolittle and the Dodgen's were about three-miles from the Dodgen's office, the sheriff's secretary reached him on his radio and told him that the owner of the old abattoir property was listed as Sammy Paul, no middle name or initial given. Hilton smiled and said, "I should have been able to recall that name, because I remember now that I mentioned to Daryl that the buyer had two first names." After a chuckle, Daryl said, "I reckon I'm getting forgetful, too, Dad, because now, I really do remember your making that remark; it was after we got back to th'office."

When sheriff Doolittle was back in his office, he called Newberry County Sheriff Bo Chrisley and asked if he knew a man in Silverstreet by the name of Sammy Paul. Sheriff Chrisley confirmed that he knew Sammy very well, and followed that up by telling Sheriff Doolittle that Sammy was in Self Memorial Hospital right there in Greenwood, where he had been in a coma for eight days. Sheriff Doolittle said, “What’s wrong with’im, Bo?”

“His van was t-boned under the traffic light at the main intersection in Ninety Six on Monday of last week; I’m surprised you didn’t know about that, Gordon.”

“He must be the one who was t-boned by a Fleetwood Cadillac driven by a ninety-four year-old woman who’s known all over Greenwood County as Ms. Money-Bags.”

“I don’t know about the Ms. Money-Bags part; but I can tell’ya Sammy has had more bad-luck in the past two-weeks than most people have in a lifetime.”

“What kind’a bad luck, Bo?”

“On Wednesday afternoon of the week before-last, the eighteen year-old daughter of Sammy and Lula Mae Paul was viciously raped and murdered about seven-miles from Newberry, out off highway-121 south, the Saluda highway. Its being investigated by my office and by SLED, but no arrest has been made; but we’re looking for two black guys, early twenties; reportedly a couple of real smart-asses.

“The Dodge automobile they were driving was found in the parking lot of a strip-shopping-center on the east side of Newberry. It’s registered to a man named Willie Artavious Spencer, 595 Sunflower Lane, Saluda, SC. Spencer says that his twenty-one year old son, and his nephew from New Jersey, Newark I think, also twenty-one, dropped him off at his place of employment before eight o’clock on Monday morning of last week. They were supposed to pick him up at four o’clock, but they didn’t show-up.

“Then, the next day a search for the car and the twenty-one year-olds turned-up the car they were driving in the strip-shopping center parking lot. My chief investigator talked with a young woman who works in a restaurant there and she said they had been in, but left between nine-thirty and ten-o’clock, and that was the last time they were seen.”

"Well, Bo, I think you can call-off the search for the twenty-one year-olds; I believe we've got'em in the Greenwood County Morgue."

"They're dead?!"

After a light chuckle, Sheriff Doolittle said,

"Bo, we don't take'em to th'morgue unless they're dead."

"How did they die, Gordon?"

"I would say—scared crapless; seriously though, they died very slowly, extremely painfully, and after hearing you say what they most likely did to justify being killed, and especially the way they were killed, they must have died thinking that they sure as hell would like to have that day to live over. But to answer your question of how they died, Bo; you really ought to take a ride up here and see for yourself—otherwise you might never believe it."

"Gordon, I'm simultaneously getting out my car keys and putting on my hat, so I'll be in your office in about thirty-minutes."

"Thirty-minutes?!, Bo, you do know its thirty-nine miles from Newberry to Greenwood—don't'cha?"

"I'll have th'blue-light on, Gordon—and I'm sure you know I'm licensed to use it! Man, you've really got my curiosity up. See'ya shortly. Bye!"

Sheriff Doolittle asked his secretary to call the hospital and inquire about a patient by the name of Sammy Paul; to ask about his condition, and to put a "Do not dismiss notice on him", and to notify the sheriff's office, if and when he comes out of the coma.

Sheriff Doolittle answered the tap-tap-tap on his door with, "Come in."

When he looked up and saw the long, tall sheriff of Newberry County, Bo Chrisley, standing in his office door, he looked at his watch, shook it a time or two and looked at it again; and confirmed to himself that the expired time since he and Bo had hung up the phone was just twenty-eight minutes. While Sheriff Doolittle stood there shaking his head, Sheriff Bo Chrisley had a grin on his face that Sheriff Doolittle interpreted as, “Don’t tell me I can’t do something—because then I’ll have to show’ya that I can.”

After a handshake, both sheriffs went to the morgue, and although Sheriff Doolittle, on the way there, had warned Sheriff Chrisley that what he was about to see was very likely more gruesome than anything he had ever seen in his entire career. And then, as they walked across the building and down the steps to the door of the morgue, Sheriff Doolittle cautioned Sheriff Chrisley again, “Bo, I promise you that the image of what you’re about to see will stick with you for the rest of your life.”

When the Greenwood County Medical Examiner, Dr. John Wallace, pulled the sheet down to the knees of the first corpse, Sheriff Doolittle was looking directly at Sheriff Chrisley’s face, and the moment the sheet came off, Sheriff Chrisley’s face, according to Sheriff Doolittle’s later recollection, momentarily froze; and his face looked ashen for at least a full-minute. Then, as he pulled the sheet from the second corpse, Dr. Wallace said, “Ditto”.

Sheriff Doolittle, “Bo, whatta’ya think’a that?”

Sheriff Chrisley, “I think th’man who did this is a stickler for detail; they’re both done exactly the same.”

Sheriff Doolittle, “That’s exactly what Doctor Wallace said when he first saw them.”

When driving back to Sheriff Doolittle’s office, Sheriff Chrisley, with tongue-in-cheek, said, “Gordon, do you have any suspects in mind?” Sheriff Doolittle, “If it turns-out that they raped and killed Sammy Paul’s daughter, it would suit me just fine for it to be ruled a case of double-suicide. But if that doesn’t work out, maybe the judge could see his way clear to sentence Sammy to life in prison, suspended for time spent in the hospital, and a month of probation." Sheriff Chrisley got a huge laugh from that suggestion.

"Gordon, knowing Sammy as I do, I predict that he'll plead guilty instead of putting his wife, Lula Mae, through the agony of a trial, during which, if it did go to trial, Sammy would admit that he did it—because those rotten bastards killed their daughter, and that if he had it all to go through again, he would do what he did, and maybe a lot more; that's Sammy, Gordon. Now I'll tell'ya something else; if it had been my daughter they did that to, when I got through with'em, DNA would have been the only way to identify their lousy, rotten bodies; because there wouldn't have been a piece of them large enough to identify. Gordon, I guess that by now you must think I'm on Sammy's side, and that I'll do anything I can to help him."

With a wide smile on his face, Sheriff Doolittle said, "Bo, it kinda' sounds that way; but all I have to say about that is this: me too."

CHAPTER NINE

Two weeks to the day after Sammy's wreck that put him in the hospital in a comatose state, he came out of the coma, and his first words were, "How long have I been here?" And when told that it had been two weeks, shock was written all over his face, and he asked the nurse if she was joking, and when she assured him that she wasn't joking, she told Sammy that she would be right back. She went to the nurse's station and told the charge nurse, Mrs. Wiggins, that the patient who had been comatose for two weeks was now awake and asking questions.

Mrs. Wiggins told the LPN to go back to the patient's room and make sure he stayed in bed—and she then called the sheriff's office to comply with his order that he be notified when the patient regained consciousness. She then went to Sammy's room and told him that his doctor had been notified, and he would be there within the hour. Sheriff Doolittle called back to the hospital and asked to speak with Mrs. Wiggins, and when she picked up, the sheriff asked her to remind Dr. Jackson to call Sheriff Doolittle.

When Dr. Jackson completed his examination of Sammy, he said, "Mr. Paul, you're a very lucky man; you could have been killed by the blow to your head that caused your coma. I'm going to keep you here four or five more days for observation. The swelling to the right side of your head, caused by blunt force, has subsided considerably, and I'm very pleased by that. I'll be back in tomorrow, Mr. Paul."

When Dr. Jackson stopped by the nurses' station, Mrs. Wiggins gave him the call-slip from Sheriff Doolittle.

CHAPTER TEN

The following morning, Sammy Paul called his attorney, Alvin Wham, and requested that he come to his hospital room as soon as possible.

At two-thirty, attorney Alvin Wham entered Sammy's room, and was quickly brought up to date on Sammy's close-call under the traffic light in Ninety Six. Then, Sammy told him about the rape and murder of his and Lula Mae's daughter, Charlene. After telling Mr. Wham how he was able to quickly learn who murdered their daughter, he continued by telling him, in detail, how he had lured the two murderers into his van and taken them to his building out near the Panorama Lodge. At that point Mr. Wham reminded Sammy that he had done the legal work on that property for him.

Mr. Wham was now prepared to hear Sammy tell him that the two men were into their third week of being held captive in Sammy's building, without food or water; but he was shocked by what he was told, in gory-detail, that Sammy had done to them. It was not that he, under the same circumstances, would not have wanted to do to the murderers what Sammy had done; but having wanted to do it, and actually doing it, were vastly different reactions that were certain to result in vastly different outcomes.

He further explained to Mr. Wham that he was on the way to his office to tell him what he had done when his van was smashed into under the main traffic-light in Ninety Six. Mr. Wham acknowledged that his secretary had told him that Mr. Paul was on his way there to see him, and that they had wondered why he didn't come in. Sammy told his attorney that the Greenwood County Sheriff was aware of the rape and murder at Newberry, and he was also aware of what he, Sammy, had done at the old abattoir building.

Sammy further shocked Mr. Wham by telling him that he wanted a trial as soon as possible, preferably during the next term of court. When Mr. Wham told him that he wouldn't be able to prepare a defense that soon, Sammy then dropped yet another shocker on him. He told Mr. Wham that he was going to plead guilty to what he had done. And when he asked Sammy why he wanted to plead guilty, Sammy told him that he was going to plead guilty because he was guilty; but he also felt that in view of the fact that the two men he killed had raped and murdered his daughter; surely the court would take that into consideration and impose a much lighter sentence than if he pled not guilty, and instead was then found guilty by a jury.

Mr. Wham explained to Sammy that if he pled guilty he would still be required to go through the same pretrial process as he would if he pled not guilty. Sammy told him he didn't mind that, but that he would like to do whatever he could to minimize the pretrial publicity. Mr. Wham told Sammy that he would go to Sheriff Doolittle's office and try to work out something.

CHAPTER ELEVEN

Attorney Alvin Wham and defendant Sammy Paul, working together, were able to have Sammy's case placed on the docket for the next term of court, over which Judge Rose was to preside, however, five-days before court was scheduled to convene, Judge Rose, considered a moderate by most of the attorneys that tried cases in his court, had emergency heart surgery. Retired Judge Randolph C. Brewster was called in to preside in place of Judge Rose; and Judge Brewster was referred to by attorneys who had tried cases in his court as "Th' Hangin'Judge". After one day of hearing the facts in the case, Judge Brewster announced that he would pronounce sentence three days later.

Three days after his day in court, Sammy, his attorney and his supporters were back in the Greenwood County Courthouse to learn Sammy's fate. After welcoming everyone to his court, Judge Brewster asked Sammy if he had anything to say before sentencing, and Sammy said,

"Yes your honor. For the trouble I have caused my family, I want to apologize to them. But for what I did to those two men who raped and murdered our daughter, I will make no apologies. If I could have killed them more than one time, I would have. The only way justice could have ever been gotten for our daughter—was for me to get it for her, and I'm very glad that I did.

"Since the Supreme Court struck-down the death penalty a few years ago, the most that could have been done to those men would have been to send them down to Columbia, or to some other location in the state system, and let'em lay-up in there to watch television and eat three-squares a day at taxpayer expense for the rest of their lives. Your honor, the way I've got it figured is that by killin'em, I not only got justice for our daughter; I also saved the taxpayers around sixty-thousand dollars a year by eliminating two future inmates.

"Your Honor, you may be waiting for me to say I'm sorry I killed those two scumbags, but the way I see it is that when they were alive they were scumbags, but now that they're dead, they're just dead scumbags. There are just two things about this situation that cause me sorrow; number one is the fact that our daughter is dead; and we will never, in this life, see our precious daughter again, and number two is that my family has been hurt so much by losing her. I'm not a college man, your honor; as a matter of fact, I went to formal school only two years, because I had to work on my parents' farm from sun-up til sun-down. What little I know, I learned from reading books. I told you about my lack of education to explain why I can't put into words the deep-pain our family feels every hour that we're awake—all because of those two useless, lowdown scumbags taking Charlene's life just as she was nearing adulthood.

"If I had not killed those two murdering punks I would never have been able to get another night of sound-sleep, your honor. I thank you, sir, for allowing me to explain to the court why I just had to do what I did, your honor."

Attorney Wham had gotten the court's permission for several people to speak in Sammy's behalf, including: Newberry County Sheriff Bo Chrisley; the pastor of Sammy and Lula Mae's church, the Silverstreet Baptist Church; and Lula Mae Paul, Sammy's wife, who made a passionate, tearful plea to Judge Brewster that had at least half of the people in the Greenwood County Courtroom putting tissues or hankies to their eyes. Her plea to Judge Brewster was so heart-rending it even had Sammy, as strong and tough as he was, reaching for his handkerchief; but his tears were not for himself—they were for Charlene and Lula Mae.

It was now time for Judge Brewster to pass sentence, and he said, "Mr. Paul, I too, am terribly sorry you and your family have lost your daughter. But as you surely know, we are a nation of laws; but you, by your own admission, took the law into your own hands by killing those two men. In accordance with the laws of the State of South Carolina, I hereby sentence you to serve the rest of your natural life in a South Carolina Prison, without the possibility of parole.

Lula Mae's mournful wail could be heard throughout the Greenwood County Courthouse, and Sammy had to practically carry her to their car.

Attorney Wham's petition to the court to allow Sammy Paul two-weeks to settle his business affairs before reporting to prison to begin his sentence was approved. Sammy, with Mr. Wham's legal guidance, worked out a ten-year deal with the four three-man crews that he had working with him in his business; the agreement being that the twelve partners would buy the business from him and pay off the debt over a period of ten-years.

CHAPTER TWELVE

Sammy was ordered to report, on the fifteenth day after sentencing, to "The Big House", as the main Penitentiary by the river from downtown Columbia was called. He was delivered to the South Carolina State Facility at Columbia thirty-minutes ahead of the 9:00 a.m. reporting time on the order signed by Judge Randolph C. Brewster, giving Sammy two weeks in which to get his business affairs in order. As stipulated in the order, Attorney Alvin Wham was responsible for delivering Sammy to the prison.

On Sammy's first day in "The Big House", he was processed into the system as prisoner number 131313, which caused him to think that it was a good thing he was not superstitious.

On Sammy's second day there, a guard came to his cell and told him to come with him; that Warden Galloway wanted to see him in his office. The warden was a big man, six-feet five-inches, two-hundred seventy-five pounds; who had been an All-America tight-end in 1949 while playing for the University of South Carolina Gamecocks, following his service in the elite U.S. Navy Frogmen during World War II. Curtis George Galloway was born on July 4, 1926 in the family home, and was also raised there on their tobacco farm, between Marion and Mullins, in Marion County, South Carolina. He was called Curt, and his paternal grandfather was fond of saying, "Curt was half-grown when he was born." He weighed-in at fourteen pounds and six ounces and was twenty-seven inches long at birth, causing his mother to spend nearly all of the three months immediately before his birth "just lying in bed", according to Mabel, his mother, whose maiden name was Hardy, Mabel Hardy.

Curt Galloway had no problem whatsoever passing for a six-year old when he was only four, the age at which his mother enrolled him in first grade at Marion Elementary School, where she worked in the lunch-room. Six weeks before his sixteenth birthday, Curt graduated from Marion High School, and with his diploma in hand, the recruiter in Florence County had no doubt that Curt was eighteen, as he fibbed that he was when he volunteered for the navy.

Two days later, while seated at the supper table with the family, and still five-weeks short of his sixteenth birthday, Curtis George Galloway broke the news that he had joined the navy and would be leaving to report for duty one week later. Mabel, his mother reacted by fainting, but was grabbed by Curt before she hit th'floor, and as soon as she was revived, she pitched what her husband, Abner, always referred to as, "one of her-Hardy-fits".

Three months before his seventeenth birthday Curt became a full-fledged U.S. Navy Frogman, and at the end of his World War II service, the truth came out—Curtis George Galloway was, at the age of sixteen, the youngest ever member of the U.S. Navy Frogmen. Although he didn't go around talking about it, Curt was four-times decorated, twice for acts of bravery and twice for service above and beyond the call of duty.

When he received his discharge in early 1946, Curt, after taking nearly three months off to do whatever he wanted to, which was absolutely nothing, rode over to Columbia and enrolled, on the GI Bill, at the University of South Carolina. Having played football in high school, Curt, quite naturally, found himself attending the USC Football Team's practices—as a spectator.

When a twenty-year old, six-foot five-inch, 275-pound athletic-looking guy keeps showing up at football practice, there's no way he will escape the attention of the football coaches—not for long anyway. The Gamecocks head coach was Rex Enright, and it didn't take Coach Enright long to sidle up to Curt and introduce himself, and engage Curt in conversation about his past. When Coach Enright learned that Curt had spent four-years in the U.S. Navy Frogmen, he was not simply impressed—he was absolutely beside himself; he would later say, "My adrenaline-level shot right off the charts".

When practice was over for the day, and Coach Enright was having his usual post-practice staff-meeting, he said, "Gentlemen, I'm far more excited about a young man I've noticed hanging around our practices than I am about any of the recruits we've brought in this year, or any other year that I can remember. I was about to refer to him as 'that boy', but I don't think a guy who is barely twenty and has already served four-years in the U.S. Navy Frogmen should be referred to as 'a boy'; if he's not a man—I reckon I've never met a man.

"He's from over in Marion County; started first grade at the age of four, played football on the varsity for four years and graduated from Marion High School six-weeks before he was sixteen! And if you're not yet impressed, listen to this: The week after he graduated from high school, he went over to the Navy recruiting office in Florence, lied about his age, told'em he was eighteen, showed'em his brand-new high school diploma and they signed him up; and a few months later he was a U.S. Navy Frogman. I don't know about the rest of you, but that is one of the damndest stories I've ever heard.

"I'm going over to the main office in the morning and ask University President Jim Ferguson to have that guy's story checked-out. I have a feeling everything that boy—I mean that man, told me is the truth; and if it is, he's got himself a full football scholarship to this university; damn, what a story!"

Two days after Coach Enright's visit to university president Jim Ferguson's office, the president sent for him. When Coach Enright walked into his office, the president could hardly wait to shove a stack of papers across his desk to Coach Enright. The papers were copies of the distinguished record of U.S. Navy Frogman Curtis George Galloway.

When Coach Enright had finished reading the sheaf of papers that described, in detail, the outstanding record of Curt Galloway, he looked up at University of South Carolina President James Henry Ferguson, and said, "Jim, can you just imagine a sixteen-year old doing the things he is documented to have done at that age? I'm not a bit embarrassed by the fact that my eyes are about to overflow at the thought of a sixteen-year old American, half-way around the world in foreign, enemy waters doing the things he did for his country—the United States of America. Even back then, what a man that boy was!

"I'm going to be proud to personally sign to a full football scholarship that four-year veteran hero of World War II, who just last month reached his twentieth birthday; that's one for Ripley's, Jim!"

University president Jim Ferguson said, "Rex, I think we have here, a wonderful opportunity to publicly honor a World War II hero, while at the same time be getting a lot of really good publicity for the university and it's football program. In addition to all the newspapers in South Carolina, we could invite those from North Carolina, Georgia, Virginia, Tennessee and Florida. This is a story that all the newspapers should want to publish about a true war hero. I see it as a slam-dunk, Rex; truly a win-win situation. What do you think?"

"Jim, I think you have just laid out one of the best free advertising plans for not only the university, but also a very deserving veteran, that anyone could have ever come up with. We can have loads of people from Marion County brought in for the scholarship signing; and just think of the pictures that would go all over the nation about The University of South Carolina Football Team recruiting and signing to a scholarship a twenty-year old World War II Hero. Jim, I get butterflies just thinking about this."

Every time Coach Rex Enright was asked to speak at functions around the state of South Carolina, which was quite often, he never failed to tell the story of U.S. Navy Frogman Curtis George Galloway, to whom he liked to refer as: "Truly a man among men".

The guard told Warden Galloway's secretary that the warden had instructed him to bring inmate Sammy Paul to his office, and she told him the warden was expecting them, and that they should just go on in. The guard knocked and Warden Galloway immediately said, "Come in". The guard said, "Warden Galloway, this is Sammy Paul. Would you like for me to stay, or wait in the outer office?" The warden waved him off, saying, "No, No. Go about your duties. Sammy and I have a lot to cover." The guard departed out the side door of the warden's office, directly into a hallway.

Warden Galloway turned to face Sammy, extended his hand toward him, but Sammy hesitated for a moment before locking his huge hand onto the warden's hand, which was about the same size as Sammy's. Sammy didn't expect the Warden to shake hands with a murderer, especially one serving a life sentence without the possibility of parole. The Warden motioned toward a chair, while saying, "Sammy, have a seat over there. Make yourself comfortable." Sammy, although warmly greeted by Warden Galloway, was ill at ease, and it showed, so the warden decided on some casual chit-chat, and after about ten minutes of that, Sammy began to feel at ease with the warden.

Warden Galloway, with Sammy's file lying open before him, told Sammy that he had been reviewing his record, and that he was very impressed with his background, and particularly his extensive experience in electrical work. Then, he told Sammy that the department of corrections had, for over thirty-years, employed a man by the name of Ralph Styles as the maintenance electrician for the department of corrections facilities in the Columbia area. However, Ralph had given notice of his intent to retire after one more month on the job; and that he, the warden, would like for Sammy to assume responsibility for the job Ralph Styles had been doing for more than thirty years.

Warden Galloway told Sammy that he had spoken with Newberry County Sheriff Bo Chrisley about him, and that the Sheriff had spoken high praise of him, and had suggested to the warden that he review Sammy's file before labeling him a common, cold-blooded murderer. One thing Sheriff Chrisley told Warden Galloway that did not get passed along to Sammy was that if he, the sheriff had a daughter and some thugs did to her what they did to Sammy's daughter, he would have killed them much more viciously than Sammy did. And another thing that Warden Galloway didn't tell Sammy was that if someone had done that to his daughter there wouldn't have been a piece of them left large enough to identify.

Sammy told the warden that he would be happy to assume the duties of the electrical maintenance man, and offered that maybe he should start working with Mr. Styles right away in order to familiarize himself with the facilities as much as possible before Mr. Styles' retirement date arrived. Warden Galloway told Sammy that he had planned to arrange that, provided he was interested in assuming those duties.

After six-months of performing the duties of electrical maintenance, Warden Galloway called Sammy into his office and commended him on how well he had adapted to prison life; and he also told Sammy that he was well pleased with the efficiency and quality of the work he was doing as the maintenance electrician.

Sammy was without a clue as to what Warden Galloway's next proposal would include; all Sammy knew for sure was that the Warden had instructed him to wait right where he was until he returned; so Sammy barely moved a muscle while waiting for Warden Galloway to come back. Several minutes later, the warden came through a door from the adjacent hallway and took the chair behind his desk.

Warden Galloway got right to the point. "Sammy, I've been considering giving you Trusty Status; which means that you would be just what the term implies, trusted, trusted to act in good-faith at all times and to never deviate from what you have agreed to do. Sammy, is that something you would be willing to do?" Sammy was quick to reply, "Yes sir, Warden Galloway. I would like that very much." Then the warden said, "Another thing that I almost forgot to mention, Sammy, is that provided there is no electrical emergency at any of the facilities, you can have your wife pick you up here every Saturday morning at seven o'clock, and she can bring you back on Sunday evening by six o'clock."

Sammy was stunned, and he walked over to the warden and they shook hands and actually embraced, as Sammy was unable to speak, because he was so overcome with emotion; but once he had regained control, he said, "Warden Galloway, you are the fairest, most honest man I have ever been associated with on a steady, daily basis. I thank you from the bottom of my heart, and I wouldn't let you down for anything, and you can count on that, sir. You have just given part of my life back to me, and I thank you for that—thank you, thank you! I can barely wait to call Lula Mae, my wife." The warden said, "I'll step out of the office while you call her on my phone. I'll be in my secretary's office; when you're through, just knock on the door, Sammy."

About three-minutes later, Sammy knocked on the door to the secretary's office, and the warden opened the door and said, "Are you through already, Sammy?" "No sir, Warden Galloway, but you know today is Friday, and Lula Mae, she was just askin' me if…." At that point, the warden interrupted, and with a smile across his face, said, "Oh, I get'it, Sammy, Lula Mae wants to know if she can pick you up here tomorrow morning—right?" "Yes sir, she's kinda' anxious, ya'know." Then, with a wide smile on his face, the warden said, "But you're not anxious, is that right, Sammy?" And with a broad smile on his face, Sammy said, "Oh, yes sir, I'm real anxious, too." Warden Galloway, still smiling, said, "Tell Lula Mae that she can pick you up out front at seven o'clock tomorrow morning." "Oh, thank you Warden Galloway!"

Sammy returned to the phone, barely able to wait until the receiver was up to his mouth to say, "Baby, th'warden said you can pick me up out front tomorrow mornin' at seven o'clock—how's that?" "Oh Sammy, Sammy, I can hardly wait'til tomorrow mornin', I'm so happy, Sammy!" "Baby, you be sure'tu'leave the bed-covers turned back in th'mornin', cause I'm gonna'be inna'hurry, too—a real big hurry!"

CHAPTER THIRTEEN

On Saturday morning at seven o'clock sharp, Lula Mae Paul was waiting when her husband, Sammy, was let-out through a gate by one of the guards at "The Big House", the main prison in the South Carolina Department of Corrections. As Sammy was opening the passenger-side door, he was at the same time telling Lula Mae to start the car and drive from the parking lot as quickly as possible; Sammy didn't want to chance causing Warden Galloway any problems for allowing him weekends away from the prison.

When they had gone a couple of miles out the highway, Sammy had Lula Mae pull into a supermarket parking lot; where they sat for at least five-minutes with their arms wrapped around each other while tears streamed down their faces. The tears were not because of Sammy's incarceration; they were because their precious daughter, Charlene, would never be with them again; not in this life.

When they walked into their home, they looked at each other for several seconds, and then started shucking their clothes. The living room sofa was not what they preferred, but it was the best thing in sight for the emergency at hand, so that was where they started; and after punishing the sofa for about half an hour, they went to their bedroom, where they vigorously exercised the bedsprings for another forty-five minutes, before finally finishing amid loud grunts, groans, moans and other familiar sounds. Afterwards they lay encircled in each other's arms; until Lula Mae's mother called to invite them to a good old-fashioned supper that she said would be ready at six o'clock.

Sammy and Lula Mae were sitting in the swing on their screened porch when she sprang it on him, "Sammy, let's have another child—pleeeeease." Sammy was surprised by what Lula Mae said, but he couldn't forget how she had turned her statement into a mournful plea by the way she said 'pleeeeease' at the end; and to Sammy's ears it was a plea—especially the way she delivered it. Sammy said, "This is quite a surprise; will you give me a little time to think about it, Baby?" "How much time, Sammy?" "Well, at least a few hours." "Until about noon tomorrow?" "Maybe." "I'll take that as a yes—okay?" "Okay, Baby."

"Sammy, if you agree to having a baby, and if it's a girl, I already have a name chosen for her; wanna' hear it?" "You know I do; what is it?" "Rulene; do you like it?" "I love it, Lula Mae; and I know where you got it; which makes me love it that much more. Ruth Charlene will be proud of it, too. Baby, when would you like for us to place the order for Rulene?" "Oh Sammy—you don't know how happy you just made me!" Then, with a big smile on her face, she said, "Can we place the order tonight?" Sammy said, "I can hardly wait to order baby Rulene, Lula Mae; and also for her to get here and be with us; but Baby, I just thought of something—what if we have a boy; what would we name him?" Lula Mae had her bases covered, and quickly replied, "Charles, of course; that's where the name Charlene came from."

Lula Mae and Sammy went next-door for supper with her parents, Mott and Daisy Gaines, and after having thick slabs of smoked ham, with eggs, grits and Daisy's famous four-inch diameter browned biscuits that she always made from scratch, Sammy was then ready for a couple of slices of Daisy's lemon meringue pie. When they were returning home, Lula Mae said, "Sammy, after eating the amount of supper that you did, do you think you'll still be able to place that order tonight?" "Oh yeah, Baby, I'll still be able to take care of that; and then tomorrow mornin' we can place a back-up order—just in case the one we place tonight doesn't do the job, maybe the back-up order will get it done." She squeezed his hand and said, "I was already think'n that we betta' place a back-up order sometime tomorrow."

After spending more than an hour placing the order for Rulene, Lula Mae and Sammy went to sleep entangled in each other's arms and legs; both happy and satisfied with the decision they had made; and bushed from the dedication and thoroughness with which they had placed their order.

Daisy and Mott Gaines called Lula Mae and Sammy to ask if they could ride with them to Columbia to return Sammy to "The Big House" where, sadly, he had been sentenced to spend the rest of his life, without the possibility of parole.

CHAPTER FOURTEEN

Nine months and two days after Sammy and Lula Mae placed the order for Rulene, forty-three year old Lula Mae Paul delivered eight-pound four-ounce, twenty-two inch long Rulene Lula Paul at the Newberry County Memorial Hospital; and as Sammy had prayed would happen, Lula Mae delivered baby Rulene at three-twenty-two on a Saturday afternoon, one of Sammy's days at home; for which he would forever remain grateful to Warden Curt Galloway. Sammy would never pass-up the opportunity to say that Warden Galloway was the kindest, most caring and most compassionate man he had ever known.

A few months after the birth of baby Rulene Lula Paul, Warden Galloway sent for Sammy to come to his office, and when Sammy arrived, the warden told him to follow him down the hall, that he had something to show him. Two rooms past his office, Warden Galloway opened the room door and old office furniture almost spilled out into the hallway. As they would later determine, the room was sixteen-feet square and had a closet and private bath opening off one side.

Warden Galloway asked Sammy how long he thought it would take him, with the help of two inmates, to remove everything from the room and place it in a new warehouse recently built on the premises. Sammy told him that they should be able to move everything in half a day. After they returned to his office, the warden dialed a number, and told the person on the other end that he needed two men, men who could be trusted, sent up to his office, where they would be working the rest of the day; and then he added, "if the men can paint, I'll need them for two additional days".

After removal of the furniture, the cleaning and painting started, and at the end of the second day of painting, floor waxing, etcetera—the room, closet and bath looked new. Warden Galloway told Sammy that he wanted him to go to a used furniture store downtown on Gervais Street, a couple of blocks west, and on the opposite side of the street from the South Carolina State Capitol. He told Sammy to ask for Mr. Bowers; and that he would call and tell Mr. Bowers that Sammy was coming. The warden told Sammy that he wanted him to pick out a good, sound queen-size bed, with new box springs and mattress, a table about three-feet by six-feet with at least four straight chairs; also two recliners, two bedside tables, two table lamps and one floor lamp. He told Sammy that he would like to have all the items in the room by four o'clock the following afternoon. He gave Sammy a purchase order to give to Mr. Bowers, the store owner.

When all the items were properly placed in the room, the warden said, "Sammy, I've already given orders that this evening, you will be moving from the cell you presently occupy, to this room. What do you think of that?" The expression on Sammy's face when Warden Galloway finished speaking was one of total disbelief; he was speechless, and walked over and took a seat at the table. His first reply to the warden was typical Sammy.

He said, "Warden Galloway, will this not cause you problems here at the prison?" The warden said, "Thanks for your concern, Sammy, but don't worry; that's part of my job; that's why they call me warden here—because I'm in charge; so don't let it bother you." Sammy could hardly believe his ears, and he said, "Warden Galloway, I'll never be able to repay you for what you've done for me, but I want you to know that any time you ever need something done that you don't want anyone else to know about, just tell me what it is, and for you—I'll do it. Thank you, sir! Again, you have saved me; I can't begin to tell you how many nights I have not slept a wink because of the shoutin', hollerin' and cussin' that goes on down there. I'll never let you down, Warden Galloway, and that's a promise that you can count on; so help me God."

The warden stepped over to Sammy and as they shook hands, the warden said, "Sammy, in my opinion, you should not be in prison, but I can't do anything about that; however, I can do things that will make your life in here much more pleasant than it would otherwise be." Curt Galloway patted Sammy's shoulder, then pointing toward the door from Sammy's new room into the hallway, he said, "That's a good lock on that door, Sammy—be sure you use it. You never know who might resent your having this room." Sammy said, "I will, Warden Galloway; thank you, sir."

When Sammy and his two helpers were clearing-out what ended up being his room, Sammy had found a piece of one and a-half-inch galvanized steel pipe about thirty-six inches long standing on-end behind the bathroom door; and he couldn't help but visualize what an asset that pipe could be if he were attacked by an inmate armed with a knife, or maybe two or three of them at a time; so with that thought in mind, he made a simple little rack to mount underneath the box-springs of his bed to store the pipe out of sight.

Then, while looking the pipe over, he thought about what an advantage he would have if he screwed a 2" to 1½" reducing-nipple onto the threads that were on one end of the pipe—sort-of-like the knob on a baseball bat; making it next-to impossible for someone to jerk it from his hands. Then he visualized the additional advantage he would gain if he applied just a thin coat of light grease to about twenty-four inches of the unthreaded end of the pipe, making it virtually impossible for an attacker to pull the pipe from his hands. Sammy showed the pipe to Warden Galloway, who smiled and said, "That's good, Sammy—keep it handy, you never know when you might need it."

CHAPTER FIFTEEN

NOTE: TWENTY-ONE YEARS LATER, THE YEAR IS 1996; SAMMY IS 62, LULA MAE IS 62, RULENE IS 19, AND WARDEN CURTIS GEORGE GALLOWAY IS 70.

Rulene Lula Paul, age nineteen, had grown into a pretty young woman, and had completed her freshman year as a day-student at Newberry College. Her mother, Lula Mae, says she can barely tell the difference between the pictures of Charlene and Rulene; and that pleases her immensely.

Lula Mae, during the years Rulene was growing up, had told her parents, Mott and Daisy Gaines, and a close friend, that she didn't think she could have survived if she and Sammy hadn't had Rulene when they did. Charlene's death, followed closely by Sammy's imprisonment, had destroyed her will to live; and she had even gone so far as to save more than enough prescription drugs to put an end to her misery.

Sammy, for the past twenty-years, had served as the maintenance electrician for the South Carolina Department of Corrections Facilities in and around Columbia. Even though he was officially serving life without the possibility of parole, Sammy had the qualifications to perform the duties of the maintenance electrician, and that, coupled with the fact that the warden of the penitentiary was understanding and sympathetic to his having killed the rapist-murderers of his daughter, Charlene. Warden Curt Galloway had been heard say, numerous times, that if the bastards that raped and killed Sammy's daughter had done that to his daughter, he would have killed them in a much more gruesome way than Sammy did, and that he would have done it with his bare hands, too; and those who knew Curt's background as a U.S. Navy Frogman didn't doubt for a second that he could have done it, and would have done it.

Sammy, on a daily-basis, thanked the Lord every morning and every night, without fail, for his good fortune of serving his sentence under Warden Curt Galloway. Not only was he selected to serve as maintenance electrician, but he so completely earned the trust of the warden that he was allowed to leave the penitentiary every weekend at seven o'clock on Saturday morning and return by six o'clock on Sunday evening; and in addition to that, Warden Galloway had instructed Sammy to move into a sixteen-foot square room with a closet and private bath only two-rooms down the hall from the warden's office. Sammy, more than anyone, realized just how fortunate he was that Curt Galloway was warden of The Big House; however, Warden Galloway had recently told Sammy that he was seriously considering retirement, and that became a constant source of worry for Sammy. He felt that his privileges would most likely be taken away, and that upset him terribly.

Although the only person he had expressed it to was Lula Mae, Sammy felt that Curt Galloway, during Sammy's twenty-one years as an inmate, had become much more to Sammy than 'just his warden'; he considered him a dear friend—actually, in his heart, mind and soul, Sammy felt that if he had a natural brother, he would have had the same feelings for him that he had for Curt Galloway; and he knew in his heart that Curt felt the same about him, too.

CHAPTER SIXTEEN

Several weeks after Warden Galloway informed Sammy that he would be retiring soon the warden called him into his office and told him he had put his retirement plans on hold for an undetermined period of time. When Sammy was through telling him how happy he was to hear that, Warden Galloway swore Sammy to secrecy; and then told him the rest of the story.

For almost two years, Democrat Timothy Hart Lackey had been governor; after playing the anti-death-penalty-card to get himself elected by raking-in over ninety-eight percent of the black vote by misrepresenting and outright lying about what he called, “the unfairness in sentencing” that he claimed existed in the state court-system; and particularly as it applied to blacks, he said. Now the governor had started a drive to build a new, up-to-date facility to house Death-Row Inmates, who at that time, numbered sixty-three men and no women.

Then, after reminding Sammy that he was speaking to him in strict confidence, Warden Galloway continued, “The true intent of Governor Lackey is this: he is dead-set on making South Carolina an anti-death-penalty state. He has sworn that he intends to see the death-penalty outlawed in South Carolina in his lifetime. He has even sworn that he is willing to die for the cause. I would say, though, that he has a very formidable little group of very powerful people standing in his way, four of whom are filthy-rich.”

Governor Lackey had requested a meeting with Warden Galloway, during which he did everything but get down on his knees and beg the warden to “stick with me” until the new death-row facility was built and running smoothly. The warden had hung-tough with the governor until the governor offered him a fifty-thousand dollar bonus if he would stay until the project was not only complete, but up and running. The warden very coyly let the governor plead his case a little longer; until the governor finally asked if there was anything that could persuade him to stay—anything at all.

The warden told the governor that there was one thing; and the governor nearly jumped out of his seat in his haste to ask what it was. Then Curt nonchalantly reminded the governor that the state owned a fifty-five hundred square-foot beach-house on a huge oceanfront lot on Hilton Head Island, South Carolina, twenty-five miles north of Savannah, Georgia; and that if the state was willing to enter into a contract that guaranteed him two two-week stays there every year for the rest of his life—he felt sure that they could reach an agreement whereby he would stay on as warden and consultant for the duration of the project's completion. The governor suddenly jumped out of his chair, as if he maybe thought PeeWee Gaskins was creeping-up behind him.

(Note: For anyone who doesn't know about PeeWee Gaskins, the most infamous serial-killer in South Carolina history; just look him up on your computer.)

Governor Lackey walked briskly around the end of his desk and grabbed the right hand of Warden Galloway as if he was his long-lost brother; and said, "Warden Galloway, you've got yourself four-weeks a year at the Hilton Head Island Beach House for as long as you live." The warden quickly said, "Governor, let's not forget the 50-G's, payable upon completion of the facility." The Gov said, "You've got it, Curt—and you'll probably earn it, too. I'll have a state attorney prepare a draft of the contract for your approval." "I look forward to seeing it, Governor."

With business done, much to the governor's pleasure, he wanted to reminisce a bit, and said, "Curt, back when Clemson and the University of South Carolina played their annual football game called Big Thursday, during the week of the South Carolina State Fair, and always played in Columbia, every year, my Dad took me to the game in 1949; That was back when Carolina had Johnny Grambling at quarterback and the halfbacks were Steve Wadiak and Bishop Strickland; and that's when Clemson was running the single-wing formation, and they had a fullback named Fred Cone, from Pineapple, Alabama and halfbacks Jimmy Wells, from Columbia, and Bobby Gage from Spartanburg. Fred Cone went on to play with the Green Bay Packers for years, and Gage, who was a triple-threat tailback, also enjoyed a good career in the pros.

"But in this particular game, the most memorable player on the field, to me, was a big man who played right-end for Carolina. He caught eleven passes that day, but the one I remember most vividly was the one he caught near the Clemson twenty yard-line, and with Clemson leading 28 to24, he simply wouldn't be stopped; and he ran completely over five or six Clemson defenders on his way to the goal line, and with the extra-point, the final score was 31 to 28."

Curt sat on the edge of his desk with a slight, tight smile at the corners of his mouth, as the Governor placed his attaché case on the warden's desk, snapped open the top, reached in and removed a Football Program that, even at a glance, looked it's age. Governor Lackey placed it flat on the desk and opened it to a page marked with a paperclip, and on that page was the picture of a man wearing jersey number 88: And beside his picture was: Position-Right End; Height-6' 5"; Weight-272; Class-Senior; Name-Curt "Frogman" Galloway and in larger type, underneath his name was-Team Captain."

But the most important information about Curt Galloway was the paragraph below his Military Record; It described how he was able to enter the Navy at the age of sixteen; about how he qualified for the Frogmen, and the accomplishments and awards that were his during his distinguished service in World War II; all during which he was barely sixteen thru nineteen years of age. And Governor Lackey was most proud of the fact that he was able to obtain the Team Captain's autograph following that Big Thursday Football Game, inscribed as follows: "Best Wishes To Tim Lackey", and it was signed: "Curt Galloway", all scrawled large across his picture.

The Governor said, "I was deliriously happy to obtain your autograph at the age of nine; but now, knowing and understanding the meaning of what you accomplished as a U.S. Navy Frogman while in foreign countries defending America and her citizens; I must confess, Curt, the paragraph about your Military Service takes precedence over anything anyone could ever do on a football field; and I want to thank you for your courageous, heroic service to our country. I am extremely proud to know you, and to be associated with you."

"Thank you very much, Governor, I appreciate your kind remarks more than I can communicate to you."

CHAPTER SEVENTEEN

The possibility of a new building in Columbia for the South Carolina Department of Corrections was generating a lot of newspaper ink, in not only the state capitol's Columbia State, but also in the Greenville News, the Charleston News & Courier and other major dailies in both Carolinas and Georgia.

As is usual when high-profile, big-money government projects are in the making, politicians and would-be politicians start the following activities: checking the political winds, posturing, choosing sides, hiring lobbyists, holding press conferences, twisting arms and lying like hell; and this highly contested project would be no exception. However, the usual movers and shakers in the state legislature, in this instance, would have high-powered, well-connected, deep-pocketed highly motivated competitors who had absolutely no interest in the political-power that might be gained, nor in the money they could have easily raked-in from property-owners and contractors associated with state projects. These competitors very, very privately referred to themselves as "The Justice Seekers"; and they had absolutely no patience with, nor respect for, the legislators who were more interested in "feathering their own nests" than in serving their state and it's citizens.

As difficult as it would have been for the general-public to believe, there really was a secret, tight-knit, six-member committee that, within the group only, referred to themselves as "The Justice Seekers". They would remain anonymous, and their only interest truly was in seeing justice done; especially in cases where the victim, or victims, had been murdered. But at the top of their list was the very significant matter of the sixty-three convicted murderers lounging on death-row. The Justice Seekers' number one mission at that particular time was getting for the murderers on death-row what they richly deserved: about an hour in the electric-chair.

When The Justice Seekers, in their completely private meetings, discussed the latest granting of an appeal on what nearly always was flimsy grounds, i.e.: "his daddy slapped him a few times when he was just a boy" ; or, "he grew up in a home where there was no father" ; or "he started running with the wrong crowd" ; or "he didn't know the difference between right and wrong" ; or "he had ineffective legal representation" ; or just any b/s excuse to touch the bleeding-hearts of a majority of the appeals court justices was all it took to keep piling-up the seniority of the death-row old-timers; while at the same time, keeping the state-paid appeals lawyers busy. One of the residents had already been there for twenty-nine years. And the family of his murder victim wants to know: "Just how in the hell can that happen?!"

If the court ruled that a murderer's father had slapped him when he was a boy, and that that was justification to grant a stay; The Justice Seekers took the view that the boy's father had probably not slapped him nearly hard enough, and definitely not often enough. Appeal denied!

If the court ruled that a murderer started running with the wrong crowd, and that it justified granting a stay; "The Justice Seekers" took the view that no one had forced him to start running with "the wrong crowd", and in the first place, maybe the truth was that "the crowd" had started running with the "wrong one"; and one of "The Justice Seekers", with his tongue barely-in-cheek, suggested that if the murderer had killed because he was running with the wrong crowd; then maybe, to keep others from being murdered by members of that same crowd, the entire crowd should be brought in and electrocuted. Appeal denied!

Another excuse that The Justice Seekers viewed with utter contempt was; "He didn't know right from wrong". They reasoned that if the ole' boy was so far off his rocker that he didn't know killing from good behavior, then just go ahead and throw his ass in the electric chair, after all: it would be a good learning-experience for him—because when the juice hit him—he would instantly know that he really had done something wrong, dead-wrong! But it was so impressive to watch the one who didn't know right from wrong, as he dumped b/s on the psychiatrists, the appeals lawyers, the judges, the jury, the press and the other bleeding-hearts he had hoodwinked for years to keep his sorry-ass alive; however, it is doubtful that even one of the people who were then fawning over the murderer would have been able to call the name of the victim, or victims, of their latest "Devil in disguise"; disgustingly pathetic is what it is. Appeal denied!

Another phony basis for appeal that The Justice Seekers also had loads of contempt for was; "He had ineffective legal representation". During the course of a trial, especially a capital murder trial, shouldn't the trial judge be able to recognize ineffective legal representation when it is happening right there in front of him, before his very eyes?

On the other hand, maybe, now just maybe—the judge could have been sitting up there with his free-hand under his robe while thinking about how he would just love to be in the nearest hotel or motel administering justice to that delicious-looking honey who had been sitting over there in the front-row of the jury-box eye-balling "his honor" since the minute she was seated, and all that time she was thinking the same thoughts that he was thinking, while continuously crossing and uncrossing her legs to give him frequent glimpses of where he hoped to land; and "to hell with that guilty bastard squeezed up in between those two half-ass, court appointed, ineffective-defenders of the guilty at the defense-table; after all—first things do come first."

And there was another thing, too; Miss Delicious-Looking had solid, reliable information: Her fortune-teller had told her just a week earlier that she would soon find happiness, real happiness; and that it would come when and where she least expected it, so this just has to be it, however, she had not expected to find happiness the very next week, and she definitely hadn't expected to find happiness in a courtroom, and she sure as hell had not expected to find her happiness with a judge, but after having thoroughly thought it through for all of thirty-seconds, she convinced herself that "this just has to be it; after all, only a fool would question the predictions of their fortune-teller."

It would be simple enough to set-up two or three cameras and record the entire trial; and then the appeals court would have proof-positive of whether the legal representation had been effective or ineffective; and if the legal representation had not been ineffective, get the execution-chamber ready and quickly set the murderer's ass in it. However, it is somewhere between extremely difficult and impossible to provide what the defendant would consider effective representation, even if the prosecution had called half a dozen witnesses who swore, on a stack of bibles ten-feet high, that they "saw that man over there at the defense table commit the murder"! That's called a slam-dunk case. Appeal denied.

CHAPTER EIGHTEEN

Democrat Governor Lackey succeeded Governor Fisher, the two-term Republican Governor, and along with the office, he inherited the architect's plans for a new high-security facility for the South Carolina Department of Corrections, and it included a one-hundred-thirty cell facility for the division housing the state's death-row.

Word spread across the country and around the world like a California wildfire that South Carolina was replacing its sixty-cell death-row facility with one that could accommodate one-hundred-thirty, all of whom swore they were innocent, awaiting their date with the executioner. And all the critics speculated as to why the increased capacity.

The bleeding hearts throughout the fifty states, working frantically through their world-wide network quickly notified every single one of the anti-death penalty nations that the state of South Carolina, in the United States of America, must be getting ready to toughen its capital-punishment laws and clamp-down on the appeals process, and in doing so, they undoubtedly would be carrying-out more executions than ever before. They pointed to the fact that South Carolina was moving its death-row from a facility capable of housing up to sixty inmates, into a new one with a capacity of one-hundred-thirty. The critics wondered out loud why the state would more than double the size of its facility if it didn't anticipate a need for the additional cells.

Reaction to news of what South Carolina was doing was not only exaggerated in scope and intent; it also ignited a firestorm of reaction around the world. Countries that some people never knew existed were heard from; and some of the third-world countries lodging complaints already had capital punishment themselves, however, theirs differed from those of the U.S. in that they didn't concern themselves with appeals; it was doubtful that they even knew the meaning of the word; and there were reports that many of those third-world countries simply took the condemned out behind a shanty and either: cut his head off, or blew his brains out, or in some cases, beat him to death with clubs and chains; which might account for the fact that they have far, far fewer murders per-capita than we have in our "more sophisticated society"; where murderers sometimes live on death-row for up to more than thirty-years after he has been convicted and sentenced to death.

But those foreign countries probably knew, based on their experiences and observations, that if they lodged a complaint with the U.S. Government in which they condemned it's practice of executing people, even though it was done by sissy-execution with a go-to-sleep shot-in-the-arm—they might wake-up one morning and find that one, or both, of two good things had happened for them: (one) Uncle Sap had sent them millions in cash, and/or (two) Uncle Sap had a fleet of ships loaded with goodies waiting in their harbor to be unloaded; unloaded by the ship's crew, of course.

What the critics didn't mention was why South Carolina would be increasing its capacity from sixty-cells to one-hundred-thirty cells. They completely ignored the fact that South Carolina had learned of a bankrupt jail-cell manufacturer in Scottsboro, Alabama that was forced to shut-down with a hundred and thirty cells in the production line; with all of them more than ninety-five percent complete.

Jim Wrenn, a longtime Machine Tool Dealer from Columbia was attending the auction on behalf of the South Carolina State Purchasing Department for the express purpose of buying the hundred-thirty jail cells for the state's new facility. On pre-auction inspection day, his first day there, Jim met Alonzo Tellis, a scrap dealer from Huntsville, Alabama. Alonzo told Jim that a major manufacturer from Huntsville would be there to buy everything; including the building, land and three key pieces of equipment with which to set-up and operate the plant. He planned to manufacture a product there that, at that time, was being made less efficiently in one of his Huntsville Plants than it could be made in the Scottsboro plant, just thirty-two miles east of Huntsville.

The following morning at 9:45, Jim was sitting in the courtroom waiting for the auction to start at ten o'clock, when Alonzo Tellis came in and took a seat beside him. Alonzo told Jim that he and Frank Jones, the manufacturer from Huntsville had been friends for more than thirty-years, and that Frank had told him that morning that he was going to buy everything there as one lot, regardless of price, because he had an urgent need for the building, land and three major pieces of the equipment.

Due to their long, close friendship, Alonzo said that he had zero-competition when it came to buying scrap from Frank Jones' two large plants in Huntsville. Then he went on to say, "when Frank says he's going to buy something at an auction—you can bank on it—he'll keep bidding until his competition folds and walks away". What Alonzo had just said was sweet-music to Jim's ears. At ten o'clock, the door to the judge's chambers swung open, but only the bailiff came out, and it was to announce that the judge had been delayed, and that he would convene as soon as possible.

Jim told Alonzo that he was in a sweat to unload the three cups of coffee he had with breakfast. Years before, Jim had learned that by going into a restroom at an industrial plant auction, he would sometimes hear two friends or partners seated in the stalls planning strategy that might net them very large sums of money. But if he did accidentally make a noise, he would simply go ahead and make other sounds, such as whistling, and then walk over to a urinal, stand there for about a minute, flush it and then noisily exit the room, and after a few seconds outside, he would turn and come back through the door in total silence, and then walk to a urinal on the heels of his shoes; and that's what happened to him on this auction day, but on his second try, he made not the slightest sound when entering. When the friends continued talking he knew he had not been heard, and that's when he listened to their conversation.

Jim Wrenn always went to auctions fully prepared for emergencies, such as the one he had encountered on his first entry into the restroom. While standing in the hallway waiting to make his second attempt to enter in total silence, Jim removed from his folder a sheet of paper on which he had neatly lettered 'Out Of Order', and using sticky-tabs that he kept in his folder, placed the sign on the restroom door.

On that morning, Jim, on his second attempt, was standing at the urinal faking it. Now satisfied that they were alone, the friends quit talking about their families and got down to business. Years before that day, Jim had obtained from a longtime-friend, recently retired from the CIA, a tiny palm-of-the-hand size tape-recorder that his friend had stated, "can record a sparrow breaking-wind from fifty-feet away".

Using another sticky-tab, Jim stuck the tiny recorder to the lapel of his jacket for backup, and it recorded the following conversation between the friends in the stalls: Friend #1: "How was your drive up here from Birmingham this morning?" Friend #2: "I decided to drive up to Gadsden last night; stayed at a Holiday Inn out beside Interstate-59, and I knocked-off the last forty-miles this morning; how about you?" #1: "I had a good flight, direct from Detroit to Huntsville; got in there at five-thirty; had dinner at a little restaurant downtown called 'Th' Dixie Rebel', and it was damn good, too. I stayed at a Hampton Inn out on Hwy-72 west."

#2: “How do you think things will go in court?” #1: “I was quite disappointed to hear the Bankruptcy Judge had postponed the auction until one-thirty or two this afternoon; I might have to stay overnight down here, and I didn’t come prepared to stay two nights; but what th’hell can we do—he’s the judge; and the last thing I want to do is piss-off th’judge.”

#2: “How in th’world did you get involved with that damn bunch’a towel-heads up there near Detroit?” #1: “Actually it’s a Deerhorn address, slightly southwest of Detroit. I sold them some equipment about ten-years ago and they kept coming back for more; but this time some really-big money is involved; and even though I don’t like the pricks, I like their money. And now here I am involved in something with them that I’m beginning to wish I wasn’t; and the truth is, it could get messy as hell.” #2: “Well, why didn’t you just tell’em you weren’t interested?” #1: “Money, man, money! I’m sure you understand that it’s all about th’money.” #2: “Just how big is th’money?”

#1: “Oh, I can’t put a number on’it, but it’s plenty big, I can tell’ya that. Well worth a trip down here. #2. “How in th’world did a bunch’a towel-heads from Michigan ever get involved with a relatively small steel fabricating business way down here in Scottsboro, Alabama? That’s a mystery to me.” #1: “I can already tell that I’m going to have to tell you the entire story about how they just happened to get involved down here, so get ready—here it comes. About six or seven months ago, two towel-heads from the tribe in Deerhorn were headed down to Tampa, Florida, and after making a wrong-turn in Chattanooga, they ended-up in Scottsboro; but don’t ask me how the hell that happened, because I don’t have a clue. You know how well the Interstates are marked, so it took two towel-heads to screw-up that bad.

"But this I do know; the two clowns who were lost took the fact that they ended-up in a rather remote place in northeast Alabama as "a sign direct from Allah" that they were sent to form a Muslim tribe in Scottsboro, Alabama. But after realizing that they were lost, the dummies stopped at the first-place they came to and asked, "Where are we?" well, that "first-place" just happens to be the reason for this bankruptcy auction." #2: "Please tell me, Sol, how two towel-heads from Michigan got lost on their way to Tampa, Florida and ended-up in Scottsboro, Alabama at a fabrication plant asking, "where the hell are we", could possibly play a role in that plant's going into bankruptcy." After #1 quit laughing, he said: "That's a good question, Abe, and from that point on it really gets convoluted; but I'll do my best to explain it clearly.

"The towel-heads asked the owner of the fabrication plant if they could walk through and see the work they were doing, and the owner, a fellow named Bill Newton, agreed to show them through. The visitors didn't know before going into the plant that jail cells were being manufactured there. After leaving the plant, the two lost Muslims went to a pay phone and called the city hall in Deerhorn, and when the secretary quit laughing about their being lost, he put the head-bosshog on the phone, and after the towel-heads finished telling the bosshog, "we believe that Allah intervened when we got to Chattanooga and put us on the road that would deliver us here to Scottsboro to establish a tribe," they told him about touring the fabrication plant that made jail-cells, and boom!, the Tribe Chief jumped right in and told the lost-one down in Alabama: "Our Deerhorn City Jail is desperately in need of cells; we've got people packed-in our jail-cells like sardines!"

"Two weeks later, after the Michigan tribe chief's visit to the jail-cell manufacturing plant, a purchase order was issued to Scottsboro Steel Works for one-hundred-thirty (130) 8 ft. x 10 ft. maximum-security jail-cells (per the attached specifications) for a total price of one- million three-hundred-thousand dollars ($1,300,000.00), F.0.B. Scottsboro, Alabama. Terms: Ten percent ($130,000.00) with the order. Delivery: In full within 120 days. No partial shipments. Balance by wire transfer prior to shipment.

"Scottsboro Steel Works used the purchase order from the towel-heads as proof of ability to pay for the materials necessary to produce the cells, and after conversations back and forth between the towel-head tribe, their attorney, and their bank, which strangely enough was The First National Bank of Atlanta; the fact that they banked in Atlanta raised questions—questions which were immediately forgotten when Birmingham Steel and Supply Company's credit manager was told by Jack Cahill, the president of First National Bank of Atlanta, that the account about which he was inquiring maintained a balance of at least twenty-five million dollars at all times. After the credit manager recovered, and was able to get up off his office floor, he immediately authorized shipment of the materials.

"About four-weeks after Scottsboro Steel Works received the purchase order for a hundred-thirty cells; two van loads of towel-heads arrived on the main-drag in downtown Scottsboro shortly before noon. By count, there were twenty-four of them, and their arrival immediately scared the hell out of the shoppers and the merchants, especially the women-folk. People in Scottsboro were not accustomed to seeing men on the streets of their town wearing sheets for clothing, and what looked large enough to be white beach-towels wrapped repeatedly around their heads; only on television had the residents of Scottsboro seen such ridiculous-looking outfits, and they were determined to continue seeing them only on television, too.

"Word spread like wildfire; and in less than an hour there had gathered down on main street, a crowd of men that the police chief estimated to number at least two-hundred—maybe more; and every one of them was armed to the teeth, carrying a long-gun, either a shotgun or a rifle, and nearly all of them had side-arms, most in holsters strapped around the waist, but some had their pistol in their pocket with the end of the gun sticking up above the top of their pocket; the message was: "We're ready for'ya and it's time for you to get your sorry asses outta' Scottsboro!"

"Apparently the message was not wasted on the towel-heads. Word around town was that when the men of Scottsboro started moving toward the towel-heads, they nearly turned their vans over in their mad-rush to get in and haul ass. It was later confirmed that the towel-heads were so anxious to get th'hell out of Scottsboro that when headed out to Hwy-72 with six pickup truck loads of wild-eyed locals on their bumpers firing guns into the air that they overshot Hwy-72; then they crossed the Tennessee River and hauled-ass northeast toward Chattanooga on Highway-71. About twenty-miles up the road, they came to the Catchahoney Truck Stop at the intersection with Interstate-59, just a few miles south of Chattanooga.

"David Murdoch, the mayor of Scottsboro, returning from an all-nighter with one of his lady-friends in Chattanooga, stopped to gas-up at the truck-stop, and while doing so, saw the two unevenly-loaded vans park over on the edge of the yard. The mayor, who took pride in seeing and knowing everything that was happening around him, noticed that eighteen towel-heads climbed out of one van while only six emerged from the identical van parked in front of it. He thought that was odd, but what th'hell, to the mayor, anyone wearing a towel around his head looked odd, therefore he must be odd, and he was about to brush it off as such when the overwhelming roar of motorcycles drowned-out damn-near everything on the south-side of Chattanooga, and that included the loudest of the big-rigs, too.

“There must have been at least sixty to seventy bikers swarming around the two vans; and those who thought watching the muslims load into the vans down in Scottsboro about an hour earlier was something to see, should have been at the Catchahoney Truck-Stop when that crowd of bikers rode onto the yard and swarmed the towel-heads’ vans. The bikers formed a circle three-deep—all the way around the two vans.

“The driver of the first van, parked in front of the second one, had locked the doors of his van, and during his frantic, desperate search for the key, he ripped what appeared to be a king-size fitted-sheet completely from his body, and with nowhere else to go, squeezed himself into the second van as the twenty-fourth passenger in a twelve-passenger van. When another towel-head jerked the towel from the head of the nearly naked one—the key to the first van dropped from the towel.

“The bikers were having themselves a field-day as they very deliberately—in a way that they seemed to consider ‘an art form’, used huge log-chains and crowbars to break out all the windows, headlights and tail-lights, and basically destroying the two vans. When there was nothing left to destroy, the biggest, burliest, baddest looking biker in the crowd, called “Th’Beast” by his fellow bikers, stood in front of the van that had twenty-four towel-heads packed inside the twelve-passenger van and said, ‘If you odd-ball, towel-head sumbitches evva’ come back’ta this part’a th’country, an’that specially includes Scottsboro, Alabama; we’ll bring ten-times this many bikers and we’ll skin’yo sorry-asses—an’then we’ll po’tuppentine all over’ya’—an’afta d’hat somebody’jus might axidently drop’a match or a lit-cigarette-butt! Now get’cho mangy’asses outta’ d’his part’a th’world! An’don’tcha even think’about comin’back he’ah; cause’ nex’time we’won’t treat yees’ neah’as nice as wees’is treatin’ya tu’day!!’”

“For the warm, hospitable greeting they received at the Catchahoney Truck Stop, the towel-heads had ‘Biker-Bob’ down in Scottsboro to thank; because ‘Biker-Bob’, before the towel-heads had crossed the Tennessee River on their ground-flight out of Scottsboro, had already radioed his pal, “Th’Beast”, the biggest, baddest biker in the Chattanooga area, to round-up his troops and head out to Catchahoney’s to welcome two van loads of towel-heads that came to Scottsboro with plans to set-up a tribe there.

“Scottsboro’s mayor, when the bikers arrived on the scene, had immediately stopped gassing-up at the pump and moved to a safer spot on the opposite perimeter of the yard; the mayor, if charged with being a philanderer, might not have pled innocent, but certainly no one could accuse him of being stupid. The mayor had heard the ‘baddest of the bikers’ mention Scottsboro, but he would not learn what had happened there until he got back home. The mayor prayed-out-loud all the way from Catchahoney’s Truck Stop to the heart of Scottsboro that nothing had happened there that would tarnish the image of his town; but he soon took comfort in the knowledge that Scottsboro, Alabama was known and respected as a peaceful place, whose citizens were kind, compassionate, neighborly, God-fearing people. But he wasn’t about to claim that they would stand idly-by while a tribe of Muslim towel-heads moved-in to establish a tribe right there in Scottsboro, on the banks of the Tennessee River. He figured that even God would not approve of that; so why should the residents of Scottsboro approve of and allow it if God wouldn’t?”

#2 said, “Sol, that’s one hell’uva story; maybe the best I’ve ever heard.”

#1 said, “Let’s get on back to the courtroom, Abe. It would be hell’uva come-off if we sat down here tellin’ stories and missed the damn auction.”

CHAPTER NINETEEN

Jim Wrenn, at the sound of commodes flushing in the stalls, quickly but quietly exited the restroom, pulling the 'Out Of Order' sign from the door as he went.

Back in the courtroom, Jim motioned for Alonzo Tellis, the scrap dealer, to step out into the hallway with him. Jim asked him if he could cut a deal with Frank Jones, his manufacturer-friend, before the auction. Alonzo asked him what he had in mind. Jim asked him how much he was currently paying for scrap, and Alonzo told him his friend was selling it to him for six-cents a pound. Jim asked him if he would be interested in making a deal for all of the jail cells for ten-cents a pound, as is, where is; conditional upon their making and signing a "binding agreement" before the auction. Alonzo said, "I sure as hell would, and if you'll wait right here, I'll give you an answer right away".

Jim watched Alonzo as he approached his friend, Frank Jones, who at that moment was standing with three other men down in the front of the courtroom. As Alonzo motioned for Frank to step over to where he was, Jim Wrenn was thinking, "now I'm about to find out if Alonzo and Frank Jones, really are close friends". After exchanging a few words back and forth, the two men shook hands and Frank Jones rejoined his group.

When Jim saw him approaching with a mile-wide smile on his face he knew that Alonzo and the manufacturer really were close friends, and that the deal was done. And with a relaxed smile on his face, Jim thought about the guy in the restroom stall, friend #1, the one from Detroit, and how he was going to be some kinda-pissed when he learned that the ninety-cents per pound the towel-heads were willing to pay him was not going to materialize; meaning that if the jail cells, though more than ninety-five percent complete, had been sold separately and if he could have bought them for fifty-cents per pound, which would have been an extremely high price to pay for scrap steel, which is how they were advertised; the dealer from Detroit would have made one-hundred and four-thousand dollars for his two-days work; whereas now he would make for his efforts not one red cent; and on top of that the towel-heads would likely blame him for not getting the cells for them; putting him in a lose-lose position.

Jim took a sheet of paper from his briefcase and hand wrote, in it's entirety, the agreement he had with the scrap dealer, and then Jim and Alonzo went out into the hallway and found the office of the clerk of court; where he gave the scrap dealer five crisp, new hundred-dollar bills as "a binding deposit", and then they affixed their signatures before the clerk of court signed and stamped it. Jim then asked the clerk of court to make a copy of the document, which he handed the scrap dealer. After handing the wide-eyed clerk a fifty-dollar bill, Jim thanked her, and he and Alonzo returned to the courtroom. When the scrap dealer asked him why he insisted on giving him a deposit, Jim told him, "the cash deposit makes it binding, whereas a check could be returned and the deal cancelled". The surprised scrap dealer told him that he had never heard that before; and Wrenn just stood there smiling as he looked at Alonzo.

Judge Rupert P. Woodward entered the courtroom and after explaining the ground-rules, put the assets of Scottsboro Steel Works Incorporated up for sale—as one lot; meaning that everything, including the real estate, would be sold as one lot; the high bidder takes all. When all the other bidders stopped bidding, Frank Jones was the only one still standing. As he had promised his friend, Alonzo the scrap man, Frank had bought everything, meaning that Alonzo, and eventually, Jim Wrenn, would take possession of the hundred and thirty jail-cells.

The Judge dropped the hammer on the sale of the entire lot; which included thirty-five acres of prime real estate just a stones throw from the Tennessee River, and with it was included the sixty-thousand square-foot high-bay, top quality steel-building that was only six-years old, and equipped with three ten-ton bridge cranes and one twenty-five-ton bridge crane, all top-running, and a seventy-five-horsepower screw-type air compressor, and any and all work in progress, along with any other assets on the premises that might have been overlooked. The high bid was one-million and seventy-five thousand dollars ($1,075,000.00).

Alonzo's friend, Frank Jones, an Electrical Engineer, Clemson University, and currently a big-time manufacturer serving the U.S. Space Program in Huntsville, Alabama, had relocated from his native Woodruff, South Carolina in 1964. Frank was the high-bidder for the entire lot, which included everything from the real estate to, and including, the mops and brooms in the janitor's closet. He later confided to his friend, Alonzo, that if it had been necessary, he would have gone as high as two and a half million for everything.

Judge Woodward was not yet through; he still had a bomb to drop—a huge bomb; so he gaveled for silence, and said, "Ladies and Gentlemen, there are extenuating circumstances in this bankruptcy case—circumstances of which you are most likely unaware. After a thorough review of the evidence, I have concluded that a conspiracy, a despicable conspiracy, forced Scottsboro Steel Works into bankruptcy. Eight months ago, a Muslim tribe in Deerhorn, Michigan entered into a contract with Scottsboro Steel Works in which Scottsboro Steel accepted a purchase order from the Muslims to manufacture one-hundred and thirty jail-cells for them. The contract and the purchase order were for one-million three-hundred-thousand dollars ($1,300,000.00), with a ten-percent up-front deposit of one-hundred thirty-thousand dollars ($130,000.00), with the balance to be paid by bank transfer, prior to shipment, which was to be made four months from receipt of the order. So now comes the part where the wheels started coming off the wagon, so to speak.

"There is conclusive evidence that Scottsboro Steel moved full-speed ahead with production of the jail-cells, and when a progress-review, six-weeks before the promised shipping date, assured them that they were running two-weeks ahead of schedule; Scottsboro Steel notified the Muslim Tribe of the revised completion date. When a week had passed with no response from the Muslims, the owner of Scottsboro Steel called them to be sure they had received the revised completion date. The Muslim Tribe leader told the Scottsboro Steel owner, Mr. Bill Newton that they had decided they would not be following through with the project, and he abruptly hung-up on Mr. Newton.

"After more phone calls and two letters, Scottsboro Steel's attorney, Mr. Ayers, called the Muslims, but when he told them who was calling, and why, they immediately hung-up. They were notified on three occasions that this auction was scheduled for this date, in this courtroom, and it was also emphasized that their interest could be best served by their presence here today. At nine-fifteen this morning, the leader of the Muslim Tribe in Michigan called Attorney Ayers and very arrogantly informed Mr. Ayers that the tribe had an agent attending the auction today and that he would buy the jail-cells for mere-pennies on the dollar; and when Mr. Ayers explained to him that he could not, under the laws of the United States of America, conduct such a conspiracy, as they were so obviously attempting, the tribe leader said, "Have you ever heard of Sharia Law, Mr. Ayers? That's our law. The joke is on you. We operate under Sharia Law—now what have you to say about that?!"

"Mr. Ayers came to my office and told me about the call from the tribe leader, and after thinking about it for a few minutes, I asked Mr. Ayers to call the tribe leader back and surreptitiously get him to say again what he had just a few minutes earlier told Mr. Ayers. But what Mr. Ayers was instructed, by me, to not tell the tribe leader was that the U.S. Bankruptcy Judge with jurisdiction over this case was listening-in on another phone. The tribe leader stated again, almost verbatim, what Mr. Ayers had already told me, including his stupid statement about Sharia Law.

"After listening-in on his brief phone conversation with the tribe leader, I asked Mr. Ayers if he knew anything about the financial status of the Muslim Tribe up in Michigan. Suddenly, Mr. Ayers looked stunned, and I could see that a connection was taking place in his mind, and a big smile came onto his face; and then he started speaking very rapidly as he told me of a conversation he had with the credit manager of Birmingham Steel & Supply Company shortly after Scottsboro Steel filed for bankruptcy.

"Before actually beginning work on the jail-cells, the owner of Scottsboro Steel was asking Birmingham Steel & Supply to ship to them, on open-account, just over ninety-thousand dollars worth of steel and other items necessary to get started on production of the cells. When the credit manager called the Muslim's bank, First National Bank of Atlanta, the bank president told him that the subject Muslim Tribe in Michigan maintained a balance that, at all times, averaged in excess of twenty-five million dollars; and that he, the Birmingham Steel & Supply Company Credit Manager, had nearly fainted.

"Ladies and Gentlemen, what the Muslim Tribe has done to Scottsboro Steel Works is criminal, however, Mr. Newton, the owner of Scottsboro Steel would not benefit in any way if we put all the Muslims in America in jail, therefore, earlier today I issued the following order:

"Effective today at 12:00 p.m. Central Standard Time, First National Bank of Atlanta, Atlanta, Georgia, shall freeze, in the account of the Muslim Tribe of Deerhorn, Michigan, sufficient funds to pay to the account of Scottsboro Steel Works the following amounts:

(one) Two million five-hundred thousand dollars ($2,500,000.00), actual damages, and

(two) Three million dollars ($3,000,000.00), punitive Damages, (non-taxable).

"Ladies and Gentlemen, the court appreciates your coming here today; and the court apologizes for the delay in conducting the auction; but this court shall not stand idly by while someone is forced into bankruptcy by a conspiracy designed to do just that, and in this case the evidence clearly proves that was done to Scottsboro Steel Works."

Then Judge Woodward said, "Now, Ladies and Gentlemen, I have something to say off-the-record." The court stenographer turned off her machine and placed her ear-phones on the table. "As I said, this statement will be off-the-record. The fact that Muslims come into our country with the idea that they can bring Sharia Law with them, and impose it upon anyone, our citizens or their own, is laughable and downright stupid. If they expect to live by, and impose upon others, what they call Sharia Law, they had better go someplace other than the United States of America, and quite frankly, I think that is something they would be wise to do anyway.

"To demonstrate just how stupid Sharia Law is, I'll point out what just might be the most stupid of all Sharia Laws; that is their law that permits, or maybe requires, I'm not sure which, that if a daughter or sister does something to, in their opinion, bring shame upon the family, it is the responsibility of her father or a brother, to kill her. Keep in mind that we are in a courtroom, not a church; so I'm going to say something that I would not dare say in a church; and remember also that this is off-the record, and in no way is it to be construed as an official statement coming from Judge Woodward, it comes from private-citizen Woodward.

"Now here it is: this statement is directed specifically to the Sharia Law about a male member of a family killing a daughter or sister who has, in their opinion, brought shame upon the family; my personal opinion of that law is this: it is the dumbest, most outrageous, most despicable and yes, the most illegal, of all Sharia Laws. And if they plan to come to America and try to live by such stupid, ignorant laws, they had better be prepared to see their fellow Muslims going to the Electric Chair in droves, and if I ever preside over a case in which a father or brother has, in his feeble mind, saved the honor of his family by committing such a murder, he will have one hell of a difficult time trying to buy life insurance. My John Q. Citizen opinion is that he should be sentenced to about three-hours in an electric chair.

"Personally, I would vote for an amendment to the Constitution of the United States that would prohibit the entry of Muslims into our country—for any reason whatsoever."

Judge Woodward thanked his audience for their attention, wished them well, and at the request of a lady in the audience, agreed to come down from the podium and shake hands with anyone who wished to do so; and everyone in the Courtroom stayed to shake his hand; confirmation that every person in that courtroom agreed with his off-the-record statements.

CHAPTER TWENTY

Jim Wrenn obtained Alonzo Tellis' bank transfer instructions the afternoon of the auction, and the following morning twenty-five thousand five-hundred dollars were transferred to Lonzo's Scrap in Huntsville, Alabama, and that, plus the five-hundred dollar deposit, paid the account in full.

Alonzo Tellis found Jim Wrenn standing in the hallway, just outside the courtroom door, talking with a good-looking secretary from the Clerk of Court's office about something 'far removed' from jail cells. Jim, sensing that Alonzo wanted to speak with him, asked the secretary to excuse him for a minute and turned to Alonzo, who said, "Jim, you'll never guess who approached Frank Jones about the jail cells." "Who?" "Some dude from Detroit; just walked up to Frank and said, 'I'll be glad to take those ole' half-finished jail-cells off your hands for scrap price—ya' interested?', and Frank told him, 'If I hadn't already sold them I'd be interested.', and the dude said, 'You mean you've sold them since the judge knocked'em down to you?', and Frank said, 'No. I sold'em before the auction.', and the dude said, 'How could you sell something you didn't own?', and Frank said, 'It was a conditional sale; I sold'em on the condition that if I bought everything in the auction, I would sell them to him.' And the dude said, 'For how much?', and Frank said, 'That's confidential.' "Then the dude just turned and walked away; how ya'like that, Jim?" "I like that good, Alonzo; let'im haul his ass on back up to Detroit. He's down here to try to buy'em for the towel-heads anyway." "You think so?" "No, I don't think so—I know so." "How'ya know that, Jim?" "Restroom gossip, Alonzo, restroom gossip."

Jim turned back to the good-looking secretary, and took-up where they had left off. “I'm sorry about that interruption, Shirley. Where were we when Alonzo walked up?” “We were talking about going out to dinner tonight.” “Oh yeah, I was telling you that I checked out of the hotel this morning, and that I'd have to call and ask if I can get back in this evening.” With a hint of embarrassment on her face, Shirley said, “I have two bedrooms; and you're welcome to use one of them. ”You sure it wouldn't be an imposition?” “I'm sure.” “What time will you be going home?” While glancing at the clock over the water fountain, Shirley said, “I'll be going directly home—about eighteen minutes from now. You can follow me. Where are you parked? Which side of the building, east or west?” “I'm on the west side.” “Meet me on the ground-floor, west side entrance; about five minutes after five.” “I'll be there, Shirley.”

As Shirley walked away from Jim, headed down the hall toward her office, he was mesmerized by the rear-end action in her snug-fitting skirt. He couldn't refrain from visualizing that same action in a bed later in the evening, after being fueled by three or four glasses of wine. The next morning, after spending nearly all night taming what caused Shirley's skirt to move as it had in the hallway of the courthouse the afternoon before, Jim Wrenn, after only two-hours sleep, left Shirley standing in the doorway of her apartment at seven-fifteen with a huge smile parting her lips. He then headed back over Sand Mountain toward Fort Payne, Alabama. He was busily trying to think of an excuse to return to Scottsboro right away.

South Carolina had the cells moved to a machining and fabricating shop in Columbia, ironically, on Shop Road, where they had the finishing touches added before being assembled and then delivered to a state warehouse just four blocks from the building site, also on Shop Road.

The target date for completion of the facility had been twelve months, but with the weatherman's cooperation, ten months and ten days after breaking ground, Emmett Cox, president of Architects, Engineers and Associates, of Charleston, and also chairman of the South Carolina Republican Party, in a dignified, but somber ceremony, presented Democrat Governor Lackey with the keys to the new facility.

Three weeks later, the sixty-three murderers who had been sentenced to death, included one killer who, believe it or not, was in his twenty-ninth year on the-row as a guest of the state. Total cost to the taxpayers was estimated at well over a million dollars, not including the cost of providing lawyers to handle his frivolous appeals.

The total yearly cost of keeping sixty-three murderers on death-row, including attorney fees, could total around four-million dollars, or more. It seems as though a case could be made that everyone on the-row is being paid a pension of about forty-thousand dollars a year for having killed one or more people. That alone should be reason enough to piss-off the masses and start a movement to clear-out death-row.

They should be given a couple of years to prove they didn't do the crime, and if by that time no proof has been found that the accused, tried, convicted and sentenced didn't do it, give the electric-chair a test run to make sure it's ready and fit to do what it was designed and made to do, which is: (one) scare the living-hell out of the murderer, and (two) kill him as punishment for the murder(s) he committed; and to make sure he never kills another person.

And then leave the worrying as to whether or not he experienced pain and suffering to the bleeding-heart people who, by their continued objections to the death penalty are, in a weird sort of way, disgustingly signaling their "acceptance of murders" by continuing to strenuously demonstrate against the death-penalty; which says to the victim's family, "We don't give a damn about your loss, or your grief, or your suffering, or whether your loved-one's remains have been found; or your anything else. We just don't give a damn—all we're interested in is making sure we save the lives of those poor people on death-row."

And there's another factor that should be understood and accepted: A twenty-three thousand volt shot of electricity is not administered to make one feel good; its not even to make him feel warm and fuzzy; it's supposed to kill him, and kill him dead. Ideally, he would feel tons of pain; and why should he not feel pain?, and not just any-ole-kind-of pain, but very severe pain; after all, is anyone foolish enough to think the murderer gave a damn about the severity of the pain felt by his victim or victims? Hell no!

And by all means, beware of Mr. Stupid; he's the one who knows how to retrieve from a closet, or someplace, a weapon that fires real bullets; and then he loads the gun before going to the nearest mall, playground, school, kindergarten or wherever, and shoots-up a bunch of innocent people, oftentimes precious little children; just before remembering that he doesn't remember "one damn thing", in fact, he doesn't remember having ever known right from wrong; and then between the time he kills a few people, or in some cases, many people, the court appointed attorneys go out and round-up a few egg-heads who claim to be able to see inside the head of Mr. Stupid, and usually, Dr. Egghead is the one who seems to not know right from wrong. However, you can safely bet that he knows the left from the right.

There have also been reports of a Dr. Egghead being in a room with a Mr. Stupid at the courthouse, or the jail, or someplace, and when the court appointed attorneys came in they started addressing their remarks to Dr. Egghead, while thinking, based on his appearance and demeanor, that he's the defendant. So you see, the question is—who's on third?

Does this scenario make sense?: A good-ole'boy who 'allegedly', after going on a shooting spree, doesn't know right from wrong, but seems to know all about how to load guns, and where to go to find crowds, and how to systematically go from room to room in a school building, or in a dormitory, and shoot people to death—but suddenly, law enforcement appears on the scene and orders him to put-down his weapon, and he knows that in the interest of keeping his sorry-ass alive, he had better do as told, so to save his worthless keister, he puts-down his weapon, the same weapon he had been shooting people with just seconds before—back when "he didn't know what the hell he was doing".

Does it make sense to throw his butt in a jail cell and fatten him up real-good; spend thirty-five to forty thousand dollars a year on keeping him fat and happy—simply because Dr. Egghead said he didn't know right from wrong, or what he was doing? The ones who make the decisions to keep someone for the sake of keeping them are the ones who don't know right from wrong. So if the killer doesn't know right from wrong, he's a living nuisance, and is serving no purpose by being kept alive, or warehoused, as many people prefer to call it. The answer to such a problem is just around the corner from death-row; and it's called—"The Electric Chair".

The anti-death penalty crowd was making noises. One of the three highest-circulation newspapers in South Carolina headlined an article: "Death Penalty Opponents Circle The Wagons", and the details outlined in the article could be boiled-down to one statement: "Anti-death penalty organizations across the U.S. and around the World plan an all-out-fight to head-off increased-executions being signaled across the United States, and particularly in South Carolina." The article referred specifically to the one hundred seventeen-percent increase in death-row capacity in the state of South Carolina as proof that the pro-execution side had ambitions contrary to those of the anti-death penalty liberals.

Just think about it: How could all that World-Wide reaction be nothing more than the figment of one person's imagination somewhere in the state of South Carolina? So it must be reasonable to assume that the anti-crowd was fanning the flames of "the manufactured rumors" of increased executions on the horizon. Someone took the created-news that South Carolina's Department of Corrections was considering building a new death-row facility to replace the existing one, and coupled it to a rumor that state officials were considering buying the nearly-complete work-in-progress of a bankrupt manufacturer of institutional confinement equipment, which in this case was a sanitized name for jailhouse equipment.

The newspaper reporter did not bother to investigate and search to learn the full, true story before going to press, but instead, printed what he knew to be much less than the complete story, which pointed to him as a member of the anti-death penalty crowd. His half-truth story created such a furor around the world that he just sat back and watched as he received full-credit for what would later be proved a half-truth story. The publisher of one of South Carolina's largest newspapers personally wrote an article that was published not only in the in-state dailies, but also in the out-of state papers in North Carolina and Georgia.

In his article, the publisher lambasted not only the reporter who wrote the story; he also crucified the newspaper that employed the reporter, calling them "nothing more than a tabloid posing as a legitimate newspaper", and went on to say that if the newspaper employing "that trash-writer didn't fire him they were deserving of each other". A week following the publisher's article, the reporter was said to have gone on vacation to an undisclosed location, but when he reappeared two weeks later, he found an envelope taped to the door of what had been his office. Inside the envelope was a check for two months severance pay, a 'pink-slip', and a 'Dear John' letter that was brief and to the point: "Your services are no longer needed or wanted. Your self-serving, half-truth story is responsible for the loss of thirty-two percent of this newspaper's subscribers during the past ten-days. Maybe you should try the tabloids." It was signed by the publisher.

When the small, tight-knit group calling themselves The Justice Seekers got together for a special, called meeting, all of them were highly-pissed about the world- wide misconception resulting from the article written by the reporter who knew full well, before going to press, that he was going-off half-cocked. The Justice Seekers, comprised of six people, and known only unto themselves, all left the special meeting with a daring-act in mind, an act to which each of them would individually give his or her deepest thought before their next scheduled meeting; twelve-days from that night.

CHAPTER TWENTY ONE

Inquiries started pouring into Governor Lackey's office at a surprising pace, from anti-death penalty organizations and from private citizens. Most of the organizations had done their homework, and knew that the Governor was opposed to capital punishment, but they also realized that he was in the delicate position of being the democrat governor of a republican state that had capital punishment.

They wondered how Governor Lackey had pulled that off, but it was widely known all over the united states, that two weeks prior to the election, Ted Armstrong, the republican candidate who was heavily favored to win the governorship, was caught "saddled-up and riding" with a beautiful young woman he thought to be a contestant in the Miss South Carolina Beauty Pageant, which that week, was being held in Greenville's Bi-Lo Coliseum downtown on East North Street. Ted Armstrong later remarked to one of his aids that when the door to his hotel room suddenly flew open right in the middle of their session, the two private investigators were snapping pictures so fast that he hoped he would never, ever see another damn camera-flash as long as he lived.

Candidate Ted immediately went into hiding, and was not seen in South Carolina again until three weeks after the election. It was later confirmed that the woman with whom he had been caught was a stunningly beautiful professional high-fashion model from Atlanta, and that as soon as they had hurriedly dressed and thrown their belongings into their luggage, they headed to her Peachtree Street Penthouse Apartment in Midtown Atlanta, where working together, they finished what had finished Ted's gubernatorial aspirations.

While lying on her bed, just cooling down, Ted's "thought to be Miss South Carolina Pageant contestant" sat up beside him and leaned over, placing her beauties just below his chin, and after Ted had finished licking, she said,

"Ted, I have a confession to make, and I'm afraid you're going to be upset. Will you be upset?"

"How do I know whether I will or not—not knowing what you're going to say?"

"Then I'll just blurt'it out. I'm really ashamed to tell you though; and I won't blame you if you get really mad. First, I need to tell you that my name is not Kathy Lantz; actually, it's Robin Reddy."

"All I can say to that is this: the name is very appropriate for you."

"I thought you'd say something like that." And she whopped him on the side of his face with one of her beauties.

"Well, why don't you just tell me what it is that you think is going to make me so angry?"

"It started out as a joke, but it didn't take long for me to realize that it wasn't a joke. I'm getting ahead of myself; so I'll drop back. Tim Lackey, your opponent in the race for governor: his niece and I have been friends for......I think twenty-one years; first grade and all th'way through Carolina, finishing five-years ago. Her name is Hailey Lackey. She called me two days ago—all excited, and said she needed a favor. I asked her what it was; and she started beating-around the bush, and I told her it must be something awful, since she was having difficulty getting it out. Then she said she needed me to go to bed with someone, but that it really was not just any someone; that it was "someone special, very special".

"She told me about the Miss South Carolina Pageant that starts in Greenville tomorrow, but I was already aware of it—and I told her that I was. And then she told me that the man she was talking about was her uncle Tim's opponent, and that he was reallllllly good-looking, and at that point I tried to cut-in on her, but she said, "let me finish first", and she kept talking. She said she wouldn't expect me to "really do anything with you"—that they just wanted to get a picture of you in bed with a woman; and then she started soft-soaping me again, telling me that she "just knew you would really go-for-me".

"She said they would like for me to be at the Poinsettia Hotel Bar at six-thirty, and that I should go to the small booth in the right-back corner. I asked her what I was to do if it was already occupied, and she told me not to worry about that, because they were going to make sure one of their people was in the booth, and to tell whoever was sitting there that "Hailey sent me". I asked her how I would recognize you, and she said you were six-feet, around 200 pounds, and had wavy-hair that was nearly black, and that you would likely be wearing a suit with a large badge on your left lapel with "ELECT TED ARMSTRONG" on it."

"I thought you said she told you that they wouldn't expect you to 'really do anything'; what about that?"

"Well, I didn't say that she said I 'couldn't do anything', and besides that, I didn't know ahead of time that I was going to find you so sexy and appealing; don't you feel flattered?"

"No. But I do feel lucky, work-out-tired, and relaxed; all thanks to you."

"You're just kidding now, aren't you, Ted?"

"I mean every word I said, Robin; and I'm not going back to South Carolina until after the election. I don't want to be governor anyway; it's my mother's wish that I be governor. Will you have room here for me for the next two weeks?"

"I have room for you from now on, Ted."

"Seriously, may I spend two weeks here with you?"

"Of course; I told you that you could. I guess I'll have to convince you that you're welcome here." And with that she sat up, threw her left-leg over his legs, slid forward, leaned her head down toward his and put a lip-lock on Ted. What happened during the next hour or more convinced Ted that he was indeed welcome in Robin's nest.

It was printed in newspapers throughout the southeast, and beyond, that "Governor-elect Lackey had been elected by default; and that de-fault was dat-of de' republican candidate, Ted Armstrong, who, before climbing in bed with the Atlanta model, was leading in the polls by fifteen points, and in spite of what happened in that Greenville hotel bed, and the fact that he was not seen in public again before the election, Ted still lost the election by only one half of a percentage point; which was not exactly a ringing endorsement of Tim Lackey"; all enthusiastically pointed-out by the newspapers and the television commentators.

Ted Armstrong's father, Duke Armstrong, a mega-wealthy South Carolina industrialist, was himself known to have exercised more than his share of bedsprings. At Duke's country club he was kidded about buying Viagra by the bushel. He had died at the age of ninety-five, two years before Ted made his run for Governor. Duke left Ted a trust fund of more that twenty-five million. So after his misstep in politics, Ted went back to chasing women full-time; and two-years after his run for governor, the thirty-five year old bachelor was still logging bed-miles in Robin Reddy's Midtown Atlanta apartment. Robin was frequently heard say, "I'm hopelessly addicted to Ted Armstrong."

Ted didn't find it necessary to watch his nickels and dimes; and although his trust-fund was bulging with twenty-five million, his mother, already seventy-five and in failing health, had her seventy-two million dollar estate set-up to flip over to Ted upon her demise.

When Governor Lackey started receiving suggestions that the state of South Carolina permit a certain international organization opposed to capital punishment to stage a "mock-execution" in its new death-row facility in Columbia, he thought they were joking, so he treated their suggestions accordingly. But he soon received a phone call from the World-Wide Anti-Death Penalty Association Chairman from London, England who said he wanted to come to Columbia for a meeting with the Governor, and the Governor approved the chairman's self-invitation. Two-days later they agreed on a date set four-weeks out, and in the meantime, a publicity blitz was put in motion that would assure the full participation of hundreds of organizations from all corners of the world.

"The Justice Seekers" were not asleep at the throttle, though; they were silently keeping abreast of what was going on; while they made their own plans.

Sammy brought to the attention of Warden Galloway that there were some ½" thick x 6" wide x 12' long copper flat bars that must have mistakenly got thrown-in with the jail-cells when being shipped from the plant in Scottsboro, Alabama. However, the fact that the copper bars were not part of the jail-cell equipment was never mentioned, so Sammy asked the Warden if he could use some of that material on which to have his wife and mother-in-law paint beautiful flower-scenes, to be placed throughout death-row to soften the cold, hard atmosphere of the entire area. Right on the spot, Warden Galloway approved Sammy's suggestion. The warden suspected that Sammy was planning something that he, the warden, might be better-off not knowing.

The death-row facility, when viewed from a helicopter directly overhead, appeared to be a huge cross, with one of the four-arms being twice as long as each of the other three; One of the arms housed thirty-four units and three of the arms housed thirty-two units each, making the total number of cells one-hundred-thirty. The longest arm, three-hundred feet long, in addition to housing thirty-four cells, also housed the execution chamber, the electrical equipment room, a small chapel, the administration offices, a canteen and restrooms.

Sammy had twelve of the half-inch by six-inch by twelve-foot long copper bars, described above, on which his wife and her mother had volunteered to paint beautiful flower scenes to brighten-up death-row. The hallways between the cell-fronts were twenty-feet wide, making the parallel corner-to-corner dimensions twenty-feet each. Sammy, after overlapping the bars twelve inches in the middle of the hallway, had twelve inches on each end of the then twenty-two foot long bar with which to overlap the face-plate that runs along the top of the cell-bars. After drilling holes in the proper locations, he was ready to take the bars home for his wife and mother-in-law to decorate with various colors of painted-on flowers.

The execution-chamber, including the room housing the electric-chair, and the room housing the gurneys where the "sissy-executions" would be performed, were separated by the seating area for execution witnesses; requiring only that the swiveling seats be turned one-hundred eighty-degrees to view either of the chambers.

CHAPTER TWENTY TWO

When the chairman of the World-Wide Anti-Capital Punishment Association left Governor Lackey's office, a tentative date had been set for staging, on world-wide television, a mock-execution-by-electrocution, right there in South Carolina's sparkling new facility.

The Program for the World-Wide Anti-death Penalty Mock-Execution Demonstration shall be published as a public-service in nearly all the major dailies world-wide, and it shall be printed as follows: The sixty-three prisoners on death-row will continue to occupy their individual cells; the visiting demonstrators will be placed four to a cell, with the exception of one cell, the one occupied by the World-Wide Chairman. The Chairman is saving one space in his cell for someone he strongly feels should, and will, change his mind about not participating, and join him in his cell prior to the demonstration; meaning that the total number of civilian participants accommodated will be two-hundred and sixty-eight, and after including the sixty-three death-row prisoners, the grand total occupying cells during the mock-execution will come to three-hundred and thirty-one, provided the person for whom the chairman is saving a place decides to participate.

All the real prisoners will be dressed in their regular orange coveralls, but the demonstrators will wear yellow paper coveralls over their street clothes; just enough difference in color to detect one from the other. The program will start promptly at 9:00 p.m. and anyone not there by 8:00 p.m. will lose his place.

To cover expenses, all demonstrators will be charged a $100.00 non-refundable entry fee; due not later than ten-days before the event. No cameras will be allowed. The demonstrators will be allowed to keep their yellow paper coveralls as souvenirs, to commemorate the momentous occasion. To have maximum effect on the World-Wide TV Audience, everyone, including prisoners, will be required to stand and firmly grip the bars throughout the mock-prisoner march to the electrocution chamber. The lights will be flashed to signal the beginning of the march, and they will be flashed twice when the march has been completed.

Warning to visiting demonstrators: Anyone who attempts to disrupt this somber demonstration will immediately be dealt-with in a "not-so-somber-way". Remember that you will be on World-Wide Television, and you will be required to conduct yourself accordingly.

By participating in this unforgettable event, you will, figuratively speaking, be demonstrating your willingness to die so that others might live; and may God bless you for your sacrifice.

CHAPTER TWENTY THREE

Four-days after the World-Wide Anti-Death Penalty Association Chairman's visit to the office of South Carolina Governor Tim Lackey, The Justice Seekers held another secret meeting. The world-wide chairman had told the governor he had been receiving complaints from countless anti-death penalty groups located all-around the world; and that they were urging him to organize and stage a high-profile demonstration; one that would get the attention of the entire world, and bring to a close the insanity of killing people simply because they, the murderers, were guilty of killing.

The Justice Seekers were livid when they learned of the comments made by the world-wide members—especially the one about "bringing to a close the insanity of killing people simply because they, the murderers, were guilty of killing". That statement had infuriated The Justice Seekers; even more than all their other ridiculous statements combined. And to make matters even worse, Governor Lackey threw a personal bomb onto the fire.

The governor screwed-up big-time. He said to The Justice Seekers' informant, "Being the liberal democrat that I am; I must tell you that I fully agree with the philosophy of the anti-death penalty side. For years I wrestled with the thought of taking another person's life; and then, something happened that permanently solidified my opinion on the matter. My grandmother was found dead on her kitchen floor. She had been raped, and then she was stabbed seven times with a ten-inch butcher knife. The murderer was caught three days later; thanks to a neighbor who was passing my grandmother's house just as the man walked down the drive from her house.

"I attended every single minute of the trial of my grandmother's murderer, and I don't mind admitting that I could hardly wait to see his death penalty carried out. When I was a first-year law student, my grandmother's murderer was already a year past the date on which he was supposed to have been electrocuted, and I don't mind telling you that I was highly pissed because his appeal had been granted.

"I was discussing my frustration over the murderer's successful appeal with one of my Law Professors, and he suggested I go to death row and meet with the convicted man. He felt that my meeting with him just might relieve my frustration and lingering periods of anger toward him. The professor even volunteered to help me gain access to the condemned man; and I accepted. What did I have to lose?

"The professor made arrangements for the two of us to visit death-row, and two days later we went there. We were promptly escorted to a small room, about eight-feet square. The room was sparsely furnished; having only a three-foot by five-foot long all-steel table that had a lockable clamp that secured the prisoner's hand-cuffs to the table. All four of the table-legs were bolted rigidly to the concrete floor. The four steel straight chairs had cushioned bottoms; which was the only hint of comfort in the room.

"When the three guards brought the prisoner into the room and locked him to the table, they told us that they would be waiting just outside the door. The professor and I introduced ourselves to the condemned man; and in a futile attempt at levity he said, 'well, I guess you fellas' know that I'm not the warden here', and then, as if he thought we didn't know his name, he said, 'my name is Roosevelt Tinch'. We spent a little over an hour there with Mr. Tinch, and by the time we left there, I was actually feeling sorry for him. The poor man grew up in bad surroundings in a non-air-conditioned home, and his father, on the rare occasions he was home, was always beating-up on Roosevelt.

"And another thing that I found very distressing was the fact that his family had only one television set in the house for four children to watch. And even though he lived three-quarters of a mile from his elementary school, believe it or not, he had to walk both ways at least twice a week. And there was a whole host of other things that caused him to have a very difficult upbringing; and the more I have thought about Roosevelt and the difficult childhood he had growing up, the more my sympathy for him has increased.

"So I ask you, how can I possibly stand idly by while a person who has had such a difficult life dies in the Electric Chair?"

Now then; Governor Timothy Lackey has just told you where he stands on Capital Punishment. And to flip the governor from being "a strong believer in the death penalty to the soft-hearted, chicken-livered anti-death penalty crowd", all it took was one visit of little more than an hour with the animalistic-brute that killed his dear old grandmother immediately after eating a platter of food from her kitchen table. She had paid him with cash for mowing her lawn and trimming her hedges, and when he asked her for food, she gladly obliged, after which he expressed his gratitude by slaughtering her with a butcher-knife and then stealing her money and a pillowcase full of silver from her dining room.

When word leaked out, courtesy of Republican Lieutenant Governor Harry Stiller, about the governor's conversion from pro to anti on the Capital Punishment issue, most of South Carolina's voters had mixed emotions. A poll, conducted at the expense of one of the state's leading newspapers, indicated that thirty-two percent of the voters blamed Republican Gubernatorial Candidate

Ted Armstrong for South Carolina's having liberal anti-capital punishment Governor Timothy Lackey in the Governor's Mansion.

Their reasoning was that Armstrong had been leading Lackey by fifteen percentage points when he screwed-up by getting caught in a Greenville Hotel bed with a red-hot high-fashion supermodel from Atlanta, and just two weeks before election-day; but the result was the election of Timothy Lackey by only one-half of one percent—which Armstrong supporters ridiculed as "Lackey's one-half percent landslide over an absentee opponent". The other sixty-eight percent of the voters vehemently pointed-out that not only was Ted Armstrong not married; but hell, he had never even been married. But it was too late to save Ted; the hard-core church crowd had recovered Ted's fumble—and they were running with the ball. A television commentator in Charleston said it best, "The hard-core church crowd does not blame Ted 'for partaking', but they'll never forgive him for getting caught 'while partaking'."

In 1995, a group of six people, all with a keen interest in the South Carolina Justice System, got together and formed a secret, underground organization that was, and would remain, known only to its six members. Internally, they called themselves The Justice Seekers. Externally, they were unknown. The members were known only to each other. They had nothing in writing. Their rules were strict. They dared not mention the organization or its members, except to each other. Outside their six-member group, The Justice Seekers simply did not exist.

The Justice Seekers were fuming over the fact that South Carolina was being criticized, mostly by foreigners, for building a new death-row facility with a hundred and seventeen percent increase in capacity. "And now," The Justice Seekers said among themselves, "to add insult to injury, the s.o.b.'s want to come to the scene of their nosey-intrusion and rub salt in the wound. But we absolutely will not tolerate those anti-death penalty 'fruits and nuts' successfully conducting a trouble-making event to be held in, of all places—right here in Columbia—in our new facility." By all accounts, the new Governor, Democrat Tim Lackey, was cooperating fully with the World-Wide Anti-Death Penalty Chairman to have the demonstration held in Columbia.

The Justice Seekers were also stewing over the fact that South Carolina was being singled-out simply because they chose to vastly upgrade their death-row facility. The state had taken advantage of a situation that enabled them to purchase a hundred and thirty jail-cells for; believe it or not—barely more than scrap price; and no one in his right mind would have passed-up that opportunity.

The Justice Seekers, by the conclusion of their meeting, had decided that: "We shall not sit idly by and let a crowd of blood-sucking, holier-than-thou foreigners come to South Carolina and dictate to us how we punish our criminals; and particularly not our murderers." The Justice Seekers decided to meet again the following evening to finalize a very bold, or maybe shocking decision.

The following evening, the six-members of The Justice Seekers met in a private dining room at a steakhouse on Knox-Abbott Drive, just across the Congaree River in West Columbia. The group's operations director gave the following report to his five fellow members: "Everything necessary to execute our plan, no pun intended, is about three days from being in place, ready for the demonstration and mock-execution. According to a confidante of Governor Lackey, the World-Wide Chairman reported that two-hundred sixty-seven foreign participants have already signed-up and been accepted, and most importantly, they have all paid their hundred-dollar entry-fees. The governor also told his confidante that the Chairman said he expected the final count to fall somewhere between three-hundred twenty-five and three-hundred fifty, including South Carolina's sixty-three death-row inmates."

Two weeks before the scheduled event, all the major pieces were in-place, and that included Sammy Paul's installation of the copper flat bar stock that his wife, Lula Mae and her mother, had painted with beautiful, brilliant- color flowers.

The Anti-Capital Punishment Representatives from all over the World started arriving in Columbia three days prior to the big event, and an amazing number of them were towel-heads, most of whom asked, "Where can we find the most expensive hotel in the Columbia area, and can you tell me how to get to the Capital Punishment Center on Shop Road?"

CHAPTER TWENTY FOUR

The World-Wide Anti-Capital Punishment Association Chairman from London, England arrived in Columbia shortly after noon the day before the big event, and Governor Lackey was at Columbia's Metro Airport to personally greet him as he exited the plane. After lunch at Maurice's Barbecue, between the airport and downtown Columbia, the Chairman asked to see the Capital Punishment Center; and after arriving there he strutted around as though he owned the place.

As the Governor showed the Chairman through the facility, the Chairman couldn't help but notice the beautifully painted flowers that Sammy's wife and her mother had painted on both sides of the six-inch by twenty-two foot long flat-bars that formed a twenty-foot square-frame where the four long cell-block hallway arms come together. While standing there in the center of the cell-block area, the two men spoke of their hope that "there would never be an execution of even one person in this brand-new facility, regardless of how many lives the convicted murderer had taken, or the brutality and cruelty he had exhibited in taking those lives; they agreed that he should be shown love, mercy and forgiveness—but never should he be put to death".

Governor Lackey explained to the Chairman the reasons he, the governor, would not be taking an active role in the demonstration; one of which was the fact that South Carolina was a strong capital-punishment state that did not believe in just an eye for an eye; hell no, and they wanted not just both eyes; they also wanted the head that contained the eyes! So with all things considered, he would not be present during the mock-execution-march. The Chairman told him that he was extremely disappointed to hear that, and that he hoped he would reconsider and join him and the other two blokes from Britain; and that they would save a place for him in their cell. When the governor dropped the chairman off at his hotel, he promised him that he would reconsider his decision to not participate.

Before getting out of the governor's car, the Chairman placed a hand on the governor's arm and said, "Governor Lackey, be a bloke of strong principle, and join the other two blokes and me in our cell; it will be a decision you can't possibly live long enough to regret, no matter how long you live." Then, after a wink, the Chairman was gone.

CHAPTER TWENTY FIVE

By 8:30 p.m. all the demonstrators were securely in their assigned cells, but Governor Lackey was nowhere to be seen, and Chairman Will Worchestershire from London, England, and his two countrymen, one a Mr. Starr from Middlesex and the other a Mr. McCartney from Nottingham, were peeking out from behind the bars when the Chairman spotted Governor Lackey hoofing it briskly toward their cell. Speaking quietly to his cellmates, the Chairman said, “The bloke looks as nervous as if he was going to a real execution—his own.” And the three of them laughed until the governor arrived at the cell-door.

The Governor entered the cell saying, “I reckon you fellows thought I was not going to show up.” The three of them smiled and closed the door behind the governor, who upon hearing the cell-door slam and lock tight, joked, “I hope we won’t have any trouble getting that damn door open when this is all over.” Governor Lackey commended his guests on how natural they looked in their jailhouse attire, but they didn’t seem to think that was the least bit funny, as the governor was the only one laughing.

Governor Lackey looked out between the bars of their cell at the television crew making their last-minute equipment adjustments and noticed that Warden Galloway and Sammy Paul were standing off to the side of the center-court area while also observing the TV crew. The four arms of the building point north, east, south and west; with the east-arm connecting the Administration Building and Execution Chambers to the four-armed death-row cell-block; so to get from the center-court area of the four-armed building to the execution-chambers, one would have to walk east toward the administration building.

Therefore, in order to have the Mock-Condemned one walk between the fronts of every cell in all four arms, it had been decided that the route of the march would be as follows: they would walk first to the end of the south arm and back to the center-court starting point, and then into the west arm, and back to center-court, and then into the north arm and back to center-court, and to finally complete the march, they would walk east, which would take them through the doors leading from the cell-block and continue into the end of the hallway that opened into the execution chambers on the left side of the hall.

Making every effort to have the mock-execution about to unfold before them as realistic as possible, Warden Galloway read the "Death Warrant" to the condemned and the Mock-Execution march then started. The TV crew led the way, with their camera-men riding on their electric cart that was equipped with soft pneumatic tires designed to provide a smooth ride; and behind the TV crew, and officially leading the way, came Warden Curt Galloway and the Prison Chaplain, followed by two big, burly prison guards—one on each side of the condemned, who at times had to literally be dragged along the way. He was putting on his best act for the billion-plus audience that was estimated to be watching world-wide.

As the march proceeded through each of the arms of the cell-block, the occupiers of the cells were putting forth their best act; loud, crude yells could be heard not only in the front offices, but also for hundreds of feet from the building.

When the march through the first three arms; south, west and north had been completed, and the turn was about to be made into the east arm; Sammy was positioned inside the hallway that separated the prisoner cell-block area from the areas housing utilities, the execution-chambers and the offices. As he stood against the steel door that had an eight-inch square one-way bullet-proof glass in it, he could see the marchers making the turn into the east arm, and that was his signal to make his "timed-walk" across the room to the red switch box that, when activated, would set in motion the flow of 23,000 volts of DC current to every jail-cell-bar in the entire facility. Sammy approached the red, wall-mounted switch-box with great trepidation; for what he was about to do could become an extremely weighty burden to him; but Sammy had thought it through many times and decided that the pluses greatly outweighed the minuses.

Sammy had removed the high-security padlock from the switch-lever at the beginning of the march; so there was only one thing left to do. Sammy gripped the lever firmly and pushed it upward until he felt it lock-in, which was his signal to get out of there—and fast! As Sammy pushed the side-door of the building open, he cautiously looked left and right before stepping silently out into the night-air

Meanwhile, out in the east-arm of the cell-block, the march came to an abrupt halt when the lights flickered for a second or two before sharply dimming to about fifty percent of their normal level, and the loud, shrill, piercing screams that lasted maybe ten-seconds was then followed by an eerie silence, which was then followed by a frightened chatter from the march-participants and the TV crew. All the occupants of the cells were hanging onto the bars as if they had grabbed hold of them with super-glue on their hands; even the dead-weight of the victim's bodies couldn't pull their hands loose from the bars! The TV crew was going wild trying to show everything all at once to their world-wide audience

Finally, Warden Galloway, looking as stunned as he could possibly look, and realizing that the bars of the cells 'had somehow become electrified', so he ran to the Electrical Control Room. Once in there, he saw that the big red lever on the disconnect box that controlled power to the electric-chair was turned-on; so he rushed up to the switch-box and grabbed the lever, but instead of quickly turning-off the power, he stood looking back over his shoulder toward the room's entrance door while holding the lever in the on-position for another full-minute. Then he pulled the lever downward and turned-off the 23,000 volts that had continued to surge through the cell-bars and the bodies of the three-hundred thirty-one men gripping the bars.

According to the men out in the hallway participating in the mock-execution march; when the lights dimmed, which always happens when the power to the electric-chair is turned on, "every man in the cells tried desperately to pull his hands loose from the bars but was unable to do so, and stood shaking violently from head to toe; until four to five-minutes later, when at the exact second the lights returned to bright, every man in the cells suddenly released his grip and dropped to the floor like a sack of sand".

The investigation that followed would confirm that DC current was indeed used in the unexpected mass- execution, accounting for the victims not being able to let-go of the cell-bars. After consulting the log-in register of everyone who had entered the cells, Warden Curt Galloway confided to Lieutenant Governor Harry Stiller that he was 'pretty-certain' they had three-hundred and thirty-one dead bodies in the cells, including: South Carolina Governor Timothy Lackey; the sixty three condemned men who occupied individual cells; twenty-three South Carolina Legislators; seventeen representatives from anti-death penalty states in the US, and two-hundred twenty-seven demonstrators from anti-death penalty countries all over the world.

Before Lt. Governor Stiller, soon to be sworn-in as Governor Stiller, left the gory scene, Warden Galloway, looking him straight on, said, "Harry, being a combat veteran of World War II, I have seen some really gory-sights, but I'll be damned if this one doesn't exceed anything I ever saw in the Big-One; this is almost unbelievable! It's really nasty, Harry!"

CHAPTER TWENTY SIX

All the hospitals in the Columbia Region were called and asked to send every available doctor and ambulance they could possibly spare to the Capital Punishment Center on Shop Road; and those who thought to ask the nature of the problem were told, "We've got more than three-hundred dead people out here! All electrocuted!"

One TV announcer and his camera-man went into the yard to talk with people out there. No one could recall ever having seen as many doctors and ambulances assembled in one place; even the oldest of the old-timers would later be heard saying, "I have never seen anything that could be compared to this; nothing ever"! After having his minute of fame on world-wide television, he stepped back up into his tiny motor-home and closed the door.

And then, sitting up in the back of a pickup, was a man who said, "I've seen tornadoes and hurricanes, really bad ones, too, but none of'em could compare to this, not even close!" Then he turned back to the television sitting on the cab of his pickup truck, reached down between his feet, picked up a large coffee can, and spat a load of tobacco juice into it.

And then there was a very dignified lady who stepped forward and said, "I'm a ninety-three year old retired nurse; I served in World War II, and I saw some really bad things, but I must tell you, this ranks right up there with the worst of them. But there is also one more thing I want to say: all those foreigners who came over here trying to tell us what to do; they should have stayed home. Goodnight y'all." And with that said, she closed the door of her van and directed her attention to the tiny television sitting on the dash showing what was going on in the yard and inside the Capital Punishment Center, just a couple of hundred feet away.

When the television reporter thought he was through, up walked eight young women; all wearing red, up-and-out bulging T-shirts with the initials USC distorted across the front, and their white short-shorts left very little to the imagination; and he decided to find out what they had to say; so he stuck his microphone right-up to the one who looked as though she might be the "head boss-hogette"; and he was right: she reached out and grabbed the microphone from his hand, and immediately started blurting out: "We were all sitting in the lobby of our University of South Carolina dorm watching this death-march, or whatever they called it, when all of a sudden—all hell broke loose!, and to tell you the truth, it scared the crap out of everyone in the lobby! It was really awful, most of th'girls in there started cryin', but all of a sudden, someone yelled-out, 'Its happening right down there on Shop Road, just a short distance from our football stadium.' so then we loaded up in my SUV, and here we are." And with that, she shoved the microphone back to him, and it was when they walked on past that he noticed their T-shirts were not the only things bulging.

The Columbia daily newspaper had five reporters and five photographers on site when "it hit th'fan" out at the Capital Punishment Center, and because of the ban on reporters and photographers inside the building, there were media vehicles of every description all over the yard; all equipped with antennas; but there was not a single vacant parking space in sight. The World-Wide Television Audience was said to number "a billion or more". The oldtimers on-site said it was the most chaotic and disturbing happening they had ever witnessed—anywhere.

The fact that they were not allowed inside the facility for what was planned to be a mock-execution; the media had been able to interview and photograph the seventeen visitors from the seventeen

United States that didn't have capital punishment. Also available to the media, prior to entering the death-row facility, were two-hundred twenty-seven representatives from one-hundred thirty-nine anti-capital punishment foreign countries scattered all over the world.

Twenty-three demonstrators were South Carolina Legislators, nineteen of whom were members of the Black Caucus, from both the house and the senate; and then, there was a name known to nearly every South Carolinian—and that would be Democrat Governor Timothy Hart Lackey. Governor Lackey had not been planning to join in the Mock Execution, but thirty-minutes before the demonstration was scheduled to begin, the governor entered the facility and told the chairman that he had changed his mind, saying, "Hurry! I'm going to participate!"

The other sixty-three people electrocuted were all convicted murderers; found guilty by juries of twelve, and sentenced to death for their crimes; and most of them had had multiple, flimsy appeals made in their behalf; keeping their sorry-asses alive for years, some for many years; while their victims lay dead underground, or as in many cases, the location of the victim's remains would be known only to the murderer. Many of them died simply for having been in the wrong place at the wrong time. And believe it or not—many of the victims were children; fun-loving little innocent, defenseless children—shot down for absolutely nothing that could have been their fault.

The basis for appeals ranged from ridiculous to absurd; such as: "He was mistreated as a child", or "His daddy slapped him when he was nine-years old for telling his mother to shut-up", and then there's this pathetically ridiculous one of, "He didn't know what he was doing was wrong," now just tell me how some pipsqueak sonofabitch knows how to find a gun, get the ammo, load the gun, go out and find a school, a shopping mall, a church or some other place where people gather, and then shoot-up the place, killing children, women or whomever happens to be there; but how many times have you heard of one of those cowards going to a police department or a sheriff's convention to shoot-up the place?

If some jerk is capable of loading a gun, finding a place where children, women and other easy-targets gather, and shoots-up the place, killing any number of people; he is certainly capable of walking into an execution chamber and sitting down to receive a 23,000 volt dose of electric joy-juice; remember—he didn't know right from wrong, therefore he will not get any enjoyment from life, and he won't contribute anything but misery and destruction to society; and it is unlikely that taxpayers will find pleasure in supporting his sorry ass for years and years at about thirty-five to forty-thousand dollars a year; SO JUICE'EM!

The shrill, screaming media: both print and electronic, across the US and around the world, kept the South Carolina Executions first and foremost in the news every day for months; calling the death penalty criminal, barbaric, inhumane, disgusting, unchristian, unthinkable, stupid, ignorant, and a lot of other little cute words and phrases that they're fond of rolling out when it appears the murderer of the moment might just be about to get what he deserves: the electric-chair.

There are those who argue that the only way the murderer will ever get what he really deserves is for him to be turned over to the victim's family to do with what they wish; and if the punishment for first-degree murder is ever elevated to that level; then, and only then, shall justice be truly served; as it rightly should be.

Perhaps the most difficult to understand law of any in the land is the one that disallows torture of a convicted murderer who refuses to divulge the location of the body of his victim. Why should a murderer who refuses to give-up the location of the body of his victim not be tortured until he either tells, or shows law enforcement where the victim is hidden, or else he dies from the torture; and he is not likely to choose the latter option. If he is tortured properly; using various electrical devices; vice-grip pliers; bull-whips; water-boarding; stretching-devices; sandblasting of his body, immediately followed by turpentine baths; and a host of unmentionables; he will give-up the location of his victim's body. Actually, there are probably very, very few murderers who wouldn't give it up during the first five-minutes if the one administering the torture was not timid, and just went to some really serious torture right from the start.

TIME-OUT FOR A MOMENT PLEASE; THIS NEEDS TO BE SAID, AND THIS IS A GOOD POINT AT WHICH TO SAY IT; SO PLEASE READ IT. Thank you.

WHY SHOULD THE FAMILY OF A MURDER VICTIM BE MENTALLY TORTURED DAILY, EVEN HOURLY, FOR THE REST OF THEIR LIVES BECAUSE SOME LOUSY, ROTTEN, MURDERING S.O.B. REFUSES TO TELL WHERE THE GRIEVING FAMILY'S LOVED ONE IS HIDDEN? HOPEFULLY NO ONE WILL SAY "BECAUSE ITS UNCONSTITUTIONAL"-------THE CONSTITUTION CAN BE AMENDED, AND IF THAT'S THE ONLY REASON TORTURE IS NOT USED IN SUCH SITUATIONS-------WE NEED TO GET BUSY AND MAKE IT CONSTITUTIONAL. WHY DO LAWMAKERS SEEM TO HAVE MORE COMPASSION AND SYMPATHY FOR THE MURDERERS THAN THEY DO THE MURDER VICTIMS AND THE VICTIM'S FAMILY? THAT'S JUST NOT RIGHT!!!

Several weeks ago, I learned of the murder of a nineteen-year old college student in Indiana. She was murdered fifteen or sixteen years ago, by some fat a - - creep; one of those scumbags who "doesn't remember much", he says; you know the kind. He's serving life in prison (he had also killed others), but the creep won't tell the authorities where he buried the body of the nineteen-year old, so there's the family-------heartsick over losing their daughter, and unable to bury her remains because the law doesn't permit that sorry s.o.b. to be tortured in order to make him talk. If they would let me have him for fifteen-minutes, he would talk so much they would have to gag him to shut him up. You gotta' admit—right there is a law that needs to be changed—and right away, too!

Thanks, James Knox

CHAPTER TWENTY SEVEN

After Sammy had pushed the big, long, red lever on that DC Power Breaker Box upward to the on-position, he headed for the exit door like a bat outta' hell; but when he stepped outside into the fresh, cool night air he felt miles away from the Capital Penalty Center, and he assumed the appearance of a nonchalant visitor as his long strides took him across the yard to where he crossed Shop Road, and when he was safely into the twenty-five foot tall pine trees, he started jogging mid-speed toward his ride out of the neighborhood, the city, the county, the state and eventually out of the United States of America.

Sammy's mind was jumping from one thought to another and another so fast that he told himself to concentrate on swiftly reaching his ride that was to take him to a new life—along with his wife, Lula Mae and their daughter Rulene. After breaking-out of the pines, Sammy saw the runway lights at the Owens Field Downtown Airport; and now all he had to do was make his way up to the large hangar nearest the south end of the airport, where the Gulfstream G-450 Jet with long-range fuel tanks should have been waiting an hour ago, just in case the Mock-Execution time had been moved forward.

Sammy's heart skipped a beat when he saw the big hangar, but with no Gulfstream Jet parked beside it; so he continued running toward the hangar, and just as he was about half-way across the front of the hangar—there it was—on the opposite side of the hangar, with the sweet-sound of those two jet-engines whining. When Sammy got closer to the plane, out the corner of his left eye, he spotted a black suv parked up close to the hangar, and at the sight of Sammy approaching the plane, out of the suv came Lula Mae, Rulene and Daisy and Mott Gaines, Lula Mae's parents. Sammy glanced toward the plane and saw the steps being lowered for them to come aboard.

After hurried goodbyes, they told Sammy that their personal possessions had been loaded into the Gulfstream, and that it was time to go. All five of them were highly emotional as Sammy told them again that when they got settled he would contact them, but only through an intermediary; they wouldn't be able to call or write them directly, and certainly not right away. Lula Mae was wondering if she would ever see her parents alive again; with her mother already eighty-one and her father two months away from eighty-two, she had reason to be concerned.

Reid Garrison, the pilot, left the exterior lights off until they had taxied to the end of the runway. With wind not being a factor, Reid had decided to make his departure to the north, because he had been told that under no circumstances were they to depart to the south; that would have taken them directly over the execution center. Everything was closed at the airport, but the runway lights were always left on through the night. Reid had performed his pre-flight run-up before taxiing to the end of the runway. His departure was made to the north, directly over the heart of downtown Columbia. Reid planned to fly under the radar until he reached the Miami area, at which time he would file a flight-plan, using a fictitious aircraft name and number. They would fly non-stop to Costa Rica at more than thirty-thousand feet.

The co-pilot came into the cabin and asked each of the three passengers what he could do to make them more comfortable; and they lied, telling him that everything was fine, that they were in good shape. He then showed them where they could get drinks and sandwiches when they wanted them.

Before returning to the cockpit, the co-pilot handed Sammy a large manila-envelope that, when opened, revealed yet another heavy-weight paper envelope; and when he opened it, he received one of the major shocks of his life—he learned that he was no longer Sammy Paul, he was now Raoul Feliz; Lula Mae Paul was now Bonita Feliz and Rulene Paul was now Aleta Feliz. Sammy put his long arms around Lula Mae and Rulene, both of whom had moved over beside him; and while looking down at the documents he had placed on the pull-down table before them, speaking softly, said—"We've been given new identities; we're no longer Sammy, Lula Mae and Rulene—but don't let that bother you, my babies, because the main thing is that the three of us are together; not just on weekends, but every day and night we'll be together."

Lula Mae was thinking ahead, "But Sammy, how will we live, and where will we live? I'm afraid for our future. Please tell us what's in store, including where this airplane is taking us."

With his arms still around them, Sammy said, "This plane is taking us to Costa Rica, where a nice five- room furnished bungalow is waiting for us. A rental car is waiting for us at the airport; and the house and car are already paid-up for a year. We also have, in a Swiss Bank Account, one million dollars, which we can draw on from any bank in the free world. Then, after we've fallen off the face of the earth, as far as the authorities are concerned, we will be free to move to the west coast of Mexico, where another nice, furnished house will be waiting for us. That will place us within a hundred miles of the California and Arizona borders; and then your parents will be able to visit, or they could move there and live with us."

Lula Mae, now a little more relaxed and somewhat at ease, said, "Sammy, let's just take it a-day-at-a-time, okay? But there is something else I need to know, and that is: who put a million dollars in a Swiss Bank Account for us, and who's paying for this airplane to take us to Costa Rica?"

Sammy smiled and said, "I promise to tell you about that as soon as we get to our home in Costa Rica; but don't let that worry you; it's all taken care of; I've checked it out."

An hour and a half after taking off from downtown Columbia, the co-pilot went back into the cabin to tell the Paul's that they were ten-minutes north of Miami, and ready to start their climb to thirty-thousand plus feet, where they would cruise at about four-hundred fifty knots per hour, or five-hundred seventeen miles per hour.

CHAPTER TWENTY EIGHT

The Investigation at the Capital Punishment Center in Columbia, South Carolina was in high gear; having started just minutes following the mass-electrocutions, three-hundred thirty-one of them, to be exact, none of which were officially scheduled to happen. Television commentators and newspaper reporters, with tongues in cheeks, were calling what occurred, "perhaps the most shocking event in the history of the United States."

The Columbia City Police Department; the Richland County Sheriff's Department; the South Carolina State Law Enforcement Division (SLED); and the Federal Bureau of Investigation (FBI) were all on the scene, crawling in, over and around everything in sight.

The FBI had notified all airports within five-hundred miles, with International Flights, to be on the lookout for Sammy Paul. His photo and vitals were a part of the Wanted Alert.

Less than an hour after the event, they had figured out what happened, how it happened and by whose hand it "must have happened"; so to say the hunt was on for Sammy Paul would have been a major understatement. Sammy was being hailed as: the most hated man in the state by some, or the most popular man in the state by some, depending upon which side one was on. But one thing was very clear; there were no in-betweens: everyone was either for him, or against him. But a poll the next day would show that South Carolinians favored Sammy by 81 percent to 19 percent, and a national poll favored him by 68 percent to 32 percent. The anti-crowd was furious when the poll results were announced; so the following day, the anti's had another national poll taken, and this time it was conducted by a polling company that managed to always announce results that were more liberal than the other polls. The results announced favored Sammy: 63 percent to 37 percent.

A Sherlock Holmes-mind was not required to figure out that Sammy Paul, within minutes of turning-on the switch that electrified every cell-bar on death-row with 23,000 volts of hair-raising DC current, would have been on his way out of the United States. But that didn't stop the investigators from immediately going to Sammy's home, and finding no one there, then went next door to the residence of his in-laws, Mott and Daisy Gaines, who were in bed—faking sleep; and after being roused from what they described to the lawmen as "a sound sleep", actually conjured-up the courage to act a bit indignant that the officers were even there.

The lawmen, hell-bent on having some questions answered that night, actually got-up courage enough to awaken a Newberry County Judge from his sound sleep, and after telling the judge what they knew and what they suspected, were able to get his signature on a search warrant; after which, they called a locksmith in Newberry and asked him meet them at the Paul residence.

When Mott and Daisy Gaines, Lula Mae's parents, saw vehicles driving onto the Paul property, they got dressed and arrived on the scene a couple of minutes before the locksmith was able to get the door open. Mott and Daisy huddled with the Chief Investigator and asked him to have his people conduct their search in an orderly, civil manner; that there was no reason to come in and make the house look as if a tornado had gone through there. The chief agreed, and so instructed his officers. The building from which Sammy had operated his business was on the opposite-side of a very thick stand of assorted trees and underbrush, and not appearing to be a part of the Paul property, it wasn't even mentioned.

After nearly an hour of methodically going through every square-foot of the house and garage, the investigators conceded that they found nothing there to connect Sammy to the mass electrocutions at the Capital Punishment Center. The on-site Chief Investigator approached Mott and Daisy, and while looking Mott squarely in his eyes, asked him if he and Mrs. Gaines knew anything whatsoever about where Sammy and Lula Mae had gone, and without flinching or losing direct eye to eye contact with the lawman, Mott did what anyone under the same circumstances would have done; he lied as if his life depended on it.

Whether the Chief believed or disbelieved Mott he didn't say, but he respectfully thanked him and asked that he be called if he, Mott, thought of anything that might be helpful; and Mott, still playing it to the hilt, again lied through his false-teeth; by telling the Chief, "I'll contact you right away if I learn anything"; and then, he actually gave the Chief reason for hope, by asking him for a card bearing his name and phone number. Mott was a good actor—real good.

CHAPTER TWENTY NINE

Before midnight, immediately after the mock-execution gone hay-wire, Lieutenant Governor Harry Stiller refused to panic, even in the aftermath of what many were calling: "The most disastrous man-made catastrophe to strike the South since that buzzard named Sherman needlessly made his infamous 'torch-march' through the South after the war between the states had actually ended."

A meeting that Lt. Governor Stiller had called around eleven-thirty p.m., to convene in the conference room at the Capital Punishment Center at 1:30 a.m., was attended by: South Carolina State Supreme Court Chief Justice Wade Hampton Montgomery; Attorney General Elmer Wilson; State Medical Examiner Doctor Jim Pruitt; and himself, to discuss what had happened about 9:30 that night.

Chief Justice Montgomery, about whom it was often said, by those who knew him best, "Could stand in the middle of a tornado, unperturbed, and think clearly, while those around him went to pieces," stated that their first order of business should be the swearing-in of the new governor. Just as the swearing-in was about to happen, Warden Curt Galloway knocked and opened the conference room door; and after apologizing for interrupting, explained that the fumigation experts were already in the process of sealing-off the entire office area to avoid having to completely shut-down the entire facility before spraying, offices included. The Warden asked that they continue their meeting out in the center-court area; the twenty-foot square area where the four-arms of death-row meet. The warden and the four-men in the meeting picked-up four chairs and an eight-foot long folding table from a storage room in the office hallway, and carried them to "center-court", where they set-up directly underneath the huge globed-light that hung in the exact center of "center-court".

With one hand on a Bible, and one over his heart, Lt. Governor Harry Stiller, in less that a minute, leaped from being Lieutenant Governor of South Carolina to being the state's new governor; all because the democrat governor who had, two years earlier, been elected to the office by the slimmest of margins, had decided to join two-hundred twenty-seven foreigners, most of whom were towel-heads, in their efforts to influence the will of South Carolinians by boldly interfering and meddling in the affairs of a sovereign state. Somehow—it just seemed fitting that Governor Stiller, in taking the oath-of-office, led by Chief Justice Montgomery, refuted everything the majority of the towel-heads and other foreign demonstrators stood for when he uttered the last four words of his vow—which were, "so help me God".

During the meeting that lasted just over two-hours, Dr. Pruitt, himself a pathologist, recommended that about a dozen pathologists be brought in immediately, to determine and record the cause of death in each of the three-hundred thirty-one demonstrators, and to expedite release of the bodies. Two-hundred and twenty-seven of the demonstrators came from foreign countries, and they were unofficially and off the record referred to in conversation as "the meddlers".

Governor Stiller assigned a dozen people, from in-house government offices, the task of getting pathologists to the scene immediately. Dr. Pruitt ordered that the air conditioning system be run full-blast, and that several portable industrial-size AC Systems be brought in to get the temp down as low as possible before the bodies started stinking-up the place. The odor from feces was bad enough, but the thought of adding body decomposition to the mix was definitely less than appetizing.

Four days after the mass-execution, all the bodies had been released, and the death-row facility had been cleaned, fumigated three-times and then freshly painted. The doctors, who came in to help expedite processing of the bodies, said the odor in the facility was nearly unbearable; feces was everywhere, including on the walls and the cell- bars; and the odor was said to have taken on a life of its own. The last body was released at 3:48 p.m. on the fourth day after what was infamously being called; "The electrocution felt around the world".

On death-row, several noteworthy changes were glaringly obvious: all the cell-doors were standing wide-open; all appeals had been denied; and no appeals lawyers were present.

The bodies of the foreign demonstrators, all of whom were in America to meddle in the affairs of the United States, and more specifically, those of the state of South Carolina, were returned to their homeland in planes sent to Columbia for that express purpose. Most Americans, including government officials and citizens on the street as well, had little or no sympathy for the visiting demonstrators, and that applied doubly to the towel-heads. In small towns and rural communities, sympathy for the foreigners was only a nasty eight-letter word; and it simply didn't exist, and their sympathy for the American dissenters was light, at best.

Three weeks after the 'mass-mess-up' at the death-row facility, a flood of foreign protesters from all over the world converged on Columbia, and they were joined by hundreds who came in from forty-nine of the United States; with those in favor of the death-penalty outnumbering the opposition by at least four-to-one. All of South Carolina's forty-six counties were well represented from all over the state, nearly all of whom favored the death penalty.

Clarence (Bo) Simpson, from Abbeville, SC, the spokesman for those in favor of capital-punishment, took a hard-line stance when he addressed the crowd of more than ten-thousand gathered in the University of South Carolina Coliseum. Mr. Simpson stated that those favoring capital punishment felt the state of South Carolina was unfairly singled out by the opposition, and he followed up by explaining why the old sixty-cell facility was replaced by one with a hundred and thirty cells.

Spokesman Bo Simpson further stated that it was obvious that those opposing capital punishment had unfairly used the fact that the new death-row facility, with a hundred-seventeen percent greater capacity than the old one, was proof of the state's plan to vigorously seek the death penalty for all those convicted of murder, regardless of the circumstances under which the murders were committed. He fiercely denied that had ever been discussed or considered by the state legislature as a factor in determining the capacity of the new facility.

It was in his final comment to the crowd gathered there in the coliseum, and to those watching on world-wide television, that the pro-capital punishment spokesman, Clarence Simpson, dropped the mother of all public-speech-bombs on the crowd when he said, "The seventeen demonstrators sent here from what we capital punishment advocates call the chicken-states; that's those states within the United States that do not have the death-penalty; and the two-hundred twenty-seven meddling foreign demonstrators sent here from all over the world, all got just what they deserved for coming here to tell us how to punish murderers in South Carolina. That was clearly a stupid blunder on their part!"

Most of those gathered there were no doubt thinking exactly what Mr. Simpson had just said, but they were not prepared to hear someone actually speak the words, and certainly not publicly, so the crowd's reaction was a delayed one; but when they realized, seemingly all at the same exact split-second, "Hey, he really said those words!", they erupted—and stood for at least three-minutes: hooting, hollering, whistling and applauding! The anti-execution crowd was clearly stunned, and highly pissed, too—but recognizing that they were outnumbered by at least four-to-one, made a wise decision about what they should say or do; and that was—absolutely nothing!

CHAPTER THIRTY

When the sleek Gulfstream-450 Jet carrying Sammy, Lula Mae and Rulene Paul to freedom in Costa Rica, reached it's assigned altitude of forty-thousand feet, the pilot, Reid Garrison, leveled-off at a cruising speed of four-hundred fifty-knots, or five-hundred seventeen miles per hour; and through the intercom advised his passengers that they should reach their destination in one-hour and fifty-two minutes.

Lula Mae and Rulene Paul had not slept during the past forty-four hours. Sammy, burdened with all the details that he had to be certain were taken care of, had not slept a wink during the past ninety-four hours, and with his mind racing ahead to Costa Rica, their new home, he was not likely to sleep during the next twenty-hours.

Sammy drew comfort from the fact that the envelope given him by the copilot contained not only the documents in which their new identities were revealed; it also included: Costa Rica Drivers Licenses for Raoul Feliz, Bonita Feliz and Aleta Feliz; father, mother and daughter, in that order; also keys for their house and car; along with the equivalent of one-thousand dollars US in Colones, Costa Rica's Currency; more than enough to get them to a bank that will honor checks on their Swiss Account; and finally, folded maps of the country of Costa Rica and of the city of Guadalupe. Two members of The Justice Seekers had been assigned the task of selecting the city or town in which they felt the Paul family would be safest and happiest. They selected Guadalupe, a city with a population of almost thirty-thousand, that is located twenty-nine miles north of San Jose, the capitol city of

Costa Rica. San Jose, located in San Jose Province, is a city of three-hundred sixty-thousand, Costa Rica's largest.

When the Gulfstream-450 landed at the Juan Santamaria International Airport in San Jose, Costa Rica, Reid Garrison taxied to Moreno-Cruz Aircraft Services, and waved-off the fuel truck heading toward them. On approach, Reid had given a fictitious aircraft number when responding to approach control, which a few minutes later handed him off to the tower; along with the false aircraft identification. He would stop elsewhere for fuel, after departing Juan Santamaria International. Buying fuel at Juan Santamaria International would have established, beyond a doubt, that the Gulfstream Jet had been at that airport, on that day and at that hour; because the fuel service man would have seen the number on the plane and corrected it on his fuel ticket. And of even greater importance: burned into the memory of the ground-crew would have been the vision of a very tall black man and two black women hurriedly transferring luggage and boxes from a sleek Gulfstream-450 Jet into a white Ford Explorer sporting very-dark windows; and had been there in visitor-parking for six-days.

After being on the tarmac at Moreno-Cruz Aircraft Services for only twelve-minutes, the Gulfstream taxied to the assigned runway, and without coming to a stop, went into its take-off roll. Ten-seconds after lift-off, Reid turned-off his exterior lights and fifteen-minutes later prepared to land at a small airport on the northeast coast of Costa Rica to refuel at an airport manned only by a husband and wife-team who lived in a mobile home on the premises. Their main source of income was from fuel sales, and they could not have cared less about the aircraft number or the craft manufacturer. After takeoff, Reid asked for, and received, an altitude assignment of forty-one-thousand-feet. He set the autopilot for Miami, leaned back and turned it over to his copilot. After passing over Miami, Reid let-down below radar and flew directly to Athens, Georgia, the Gulfstream's home base.

As soon as the last box was placed in the Ford SUV, Sammy, with Lula Mae and Rulene watching behind them, headed away from the airport. When they came to an around-the-clock convenience store, Sammy pulled up to the front and unfolded his area map; and after locating Guadalupe, he located the highway that connected Guadalupe and San Jose. When he looked at the overcrowded cluster of highway signs at the intersection off to his right, he spotted the highway to Guadalupe, their new home to be, about thirty miles north. Sammy, with his body desperately screaming for sleep, looked at Lula Mae and Rulene, who, although badly in need of sleep, were able to return the smile that was on his face as he looked at the two women who, to him, were the most important people in the world. Forty minutes later, they were driving into the garage of their new home at 3773 Luisa Lane, Guadalupe, San Jose, Costa Rica.

CHAPTER THIRTY ONE

Six weeks after "The Electrocution felt Throughout the World", Warden Curt Galloway officially retired from the South Carolina Department of Corrections; after thirty-three years as Warden, and a total of forty-four years service to the state of South Carolina. Warden Galloway was highly respected by his peers throughout the Southeast. But unbeknownst to most of his peers was his record as a member of the U.S. Navy Frogmen, later renamed the U.S. Navy Seals. Curtis George (Curt) Galloway, who was born big, lied about his age and was sworn into the U.S. Navy five weeks before his sixteenth birthday.

When Curt Galloway went to the South Carolina Human Resources Department to make his retirement official, he asked to see a copy of the official document confirming his agreement with the state, wherein Governor Lackey agreed. When Curt had looked at every sheet of paper in the Curtis George Galloway official file without seeing the contract granting him use of the South Carolina Hilton Head Island Beach House for a total of four-weeks every year for the rest of his life, he asked the clerk where it was, and was told that she had never seen such a contract. Curt opened his briefcase and handed his contract to the clerk, and after she was less that thirty-seconds into reading it, Curt thought for sure that the clerk was going to faint. She asked Curt if she could take the document in for the department head to see. He told her, "of course you can".

When the clerk returned, she was following the department head, who was still reading as he walked toward Curt. After handshakes, during which the department head introduced himself to Curt as Jim Allen, who told Curt that he remembered, with much pleasure, his exploits on the football field and after a couple of minutes of rehashing some of Curt's glory days as an all-america tight-end on the University of South Carolina Football Team, Mr Allen asked Curt if he could make a copy of the contract. Curt told Jim that he had no objections, "make as many copies as you care to". Jim Allen crossed the room to a copying machine and ran several copies before returning with the original. After cordial exchanges, during which Jim told Curt that he would be in touch with him as soon as he consulted the legal department, the two men shook hands and parted.

The following afternoon, Curt Galloway received a call from Jim Allen; a call that pleased Curt very much. Legal had confirmed the existence of Curt's contract with the state, in which he was to have exclusive use of the 5,500 square foot beach house for a total of four-weeks, every year for the rest of his life.

CHAPTER THIRTY TWO

Sammy Paul, after being in Costa Rica for almost two months, finally thought of a way they might be able to secretly contact Lula Mae's parents, Mott and Daisy Gaines. Sammy's cousin, Lilly Wade-Skinner, Sammy's mother's brother's daughter, was married to a man named Herman Skinner, a retired career-veteran of the U.S. Navy, and they enjoyed living in the San Diego area, so when he retired they decided to make it their permanent home. Sammy was like a brother to Lilly and her two-year older sister, Lessie Mae.

When Sammy's parents, Booker T. and Pearl Paul were killed while pulling out of the Shady Grove Church driveway onto Watts Road over in Abbeville County, Arthur and Kitty Wade successfully petitioned the court for custody of fourteen-year old Sammy. After moving in with the Wades, Sammy and his Wade-girl cousins soon became more like sisters and brother than cousins, and he continued to make his home with the Wades until he reached the age of twenty and married Lula Mae.

Sammy had always kept a small book that he referred to as "my little book", about two by three-inches and about fourteen-pages, in which he kept close-family addresses and phone numbers. He had always kept it updated, and carried it in his wallet; until he was broadsided under that traffic light in Ninety Six, and lay comatose in Self Memorial Hospital for the next two weeks. Lula Mae had taken Sammy's personal items home from the hospital for safekeeping; and when Sammy pled guilty to killing the two twenty-one year-old punks for raping and killing his and Lula Mae's precious-daughter, Charlene, for which he was sent to prison for life, with no possibility of parole; Lula Mae placed Sammy's little book in the same box with her irreplaceable pictures and other small valuables.

There were days when Sammy would, after a good, hearty breakfast, tell Lula Mae and Rulene, "today is going to be a thinking-day for me, so I'll be outside in my hammock". When he told them that, which was usually about once a week, they knew to not bother him, unless it was something very important. It was on one such day that Sammy finally remembered "my little book", and he could barely wait to ask Lula Mae about it; so when she and Rulene returned from the supermarket, Sammy reached the Ford Explorer before they could get out of it. The moment he mentioned "my little book", with a smile on her face, Lula Mae told him, "If you'll move outta' th'way so I'can get outta' this vehicle, I'll be glad to get it for'ya".

Sammy quickly found Lilly Wade-Skinner's phone number and address; and he silently prayed that both were still current. Sammy and Lula Mae had exchanged Christmas cards with Lilly and Herman every year, but they had not spoken with her by phone since Sammy was sentenced, almost twenty-two years earlier; so he decided to sit down and very carefully think through how he would proceed; or even whether or not he should. He knew that Lilly and Lessie Mae were both aware of his problems that dated back nearly twenty-two years; because he had called Lilly, and when told that Lessie Mae was in the middle of a two-week visit with her, he asked that she get on an extension phone, so he was able to speak with both sisters at the same time. He wanted both of them to know exactly what he had done, and why he did it.

The sisters had cried, and sympathized with him and assured him that they loved him as if he were their blood brother, and that they always would; and in closing, they told him that they would help him in any way they could—to just let them know what they could do. Though the Wade sisters might not have been aware of it, Sammy drew much strength and comfort just from hearing their voices, and their kind words. And he knew, too, that they meant every word of what they had told him.

Sammy was now ready to accept Lilly's offer that was now almost twenty-two years old.

Sammy sat down with Lula Mae and Rulene to discuss his thoughts about how best to contact Lula Mae's parents, Mott and Daisy Gaines to find out how they were getting along, and to let them know that they, the Paul's, were safe and well. At the mention of Mott and Daisy, tears poured out of Lula Mae's eyes, and the sight of seeing her mother crying caused Rulene to cry, too. The three of them were sitting on a sofa, with Sammy in the middle, and he wrapped his long arms around both of them, pulling them up close, and sitting there in silence until they stopped crying, and dried their eyes.

Sammy reminded Lula Mae of his call to Lessie Mae and Lilly after he had pled guilty and had been sentenced, but was still in the two-week period the Judge had granted for him to get his affairs in order before reporting to prison. Lula Mae remembered that they had offered to do anything they could to help Sammy and Lula Mae.

Sammy told Lula Mae and Rulene that he was hoping and praying that Lilly and Herman still lived in San Diego, California, where they were when Herman retired from the Navy. Lula Mae reminded him that they still lived at the same address when they sent their Christmas card the past December, something Sammy had forgotten; and he reacted to that reminder as a kid would have on Christmas morning. Sammy sprang-up from the sofa saying, "Let's go to Santiago!" Lula Mae said, "Santiago—for what?!" "To put some distance between where we live and the location the call to San Diego will be made from—just in case somebody goofed-up, and the law started lookin' for'us down here." "You don't think they're already lookin for'us?" "Well, no use makin'it real easy for'em." "When're we goin' Sammy?" "I can be ready in about thirty-minutes, but ya'll can take as much time as you want; we got nuthin' else to do."

Two hours after leaving their home in Guadalupe, the Pauls were on the outskirts of Santiago, and keeping their eyes open for a bank, from which they could get a pocketful of silver coins to feed into a pay-phone. A call to San Diego, California, USA was going to require a lot of change. Sammy sent Rulene in to get fifty-dollars in silver coins. He didn't want his image to be captured on cameras in banks—or anywhere else, as long as he could avoid it.

After leaving the bank, Sammy stopped at a strip-shopping center in the next block, and got the numbers off two pay-phones.

Three blocks down from the bank, they found a pay-phone in the edge of a supermarket parking lot, just what Sammy was looking for. After placing the call through a long distance operator, it seemed as though he would never get through feeding coins into the phone; after six rings, Sammy started to hang-up, then decided to give it two or three more rings, and then, on the eighth-ring, a breathless Lilly Skinner answered, and Sammy immediately said, "Lil, don't say a word; just listen to me—do you have a pencil and paper handy?" "Yes." "Take down these two phone numbers." "I'm ready." Sammy called-off the numbers he had gotten off two pay phones on the way into Santiago. The phones were in a strip shopping-center, about fifty-feet apart, on the outskirts of town; and he asked Lilly to go to a pay-phone and call him back in exactly thirty minutes, and that if one number was busy, call the second one. She told him she would.

Sammy backtracked to the strip-center and parked mid-way between the two pay-phones. At exactly thirty minutes after ending his call with Lilly, the pay-phone on Sammy's side of their Ford Explorer rang, and he literally jumped out of the vehicle to grab it, and said, "Don't call any names, no names at all; is everybody there okay?" "Yes, what about where you are?" "All is well here. I need you to contact my in-laws and tell them that we are well, and ask how they're doing. They're most likely at home right now, so if you can, when we hang-up, call information and get their number." "Has their phone number ever changed?" "I know it hasn't changed since I've known them." "Well, I have it in my address book. I'll call them right now, and then I'll call you right back. Okay?" "Good—I'll be waiting."

"She's gonna' call them right now and then call us at this same number. Would you girls like to go in that ice cream parlor for a drink or ice cream while I wait here for Lilly to call back?" "Sammy, you know good'n well you couldn't drag me away'frum this phone with a bulldozer while I'm wait'n to hear'bout my momma and daddy; ain't no way I'm movin' til' that phone rings again."

The three Pauls must have looked at their watches every ten seconds while waiting for Lilly to call back. When the phone finally rang, Sammy almost jerked the phone-cord completely out of the phone as he rushed to answer it. "Hello, Hello!" "Just settle down, both of them are fine, but they can hardly wait to see y'all; they were like two little kids on Christmas morning to hear from y'all, even though they couldn't speak directly to'ya. They said to tell ya'll that they love you and can barely wait to see'ya." "Wait, hold just a second." Sammy placed the receiver to Lula Mae's ear and then said, "Please repeat the last thing you said to me." "They said to tell ya'll that they love you and can barely wait to see'ya." Tears literally shot out of Lula Mae's eyes when she heard what Lilly said, and at the sight of her momma's tears, Rulene also started crying and sobbing. The sight of Lula Mae and Rulene crying caused Sammy to make a quick decision—one that later, would surely shock Lula Mae and Rulene. Immediately upon hearing what Lilly said to her, Lula Mae handed the receiver back to Sammy. He ended the conversation with Lilly by saying, "I can never thank you enough for what you've done—goodbye until next time." "Call anytime." Then Sammy hung-up.

When they had been riding in silence for about twenty-minutes, headed back to Guadalupe, Sammy broke the silence by saying, "I've got to get my babies back home. I'll figure out what we can do, and then we'll call and have them send the plane to take y'all back home. It's not fair for y'all to have to pick-up and leave—when y'all hadn't done anything wrong to cause'ya to leave." "But Daddy, I don't want to go back without you." "The first step will be to get both of you back; and then I'll work on a way to get me back, too; but don't ask me how right now, cause' I haven't had time to think about that yet, but you can count'on'it; I will come back, and not as a prisoner, either. "

Sammy said, "Would y'all like to stop and have dinner on the outskirts of San Jose?" Lula Mae and Rulene looked at each other, and Lula Mae spoke first, "Baby, would you like to stop for dinner?" "Momma, I'd love to—I'm hungry." Sammy pulled in at a seafood restaurant. After they had ordered, Sammy said, "I'm going to that pay phone out in th'foyer; I'll be right back."

Sammy removed from his wallet, a slip of paper on which he had written a telephone number, in code. With his coins stacked in front of him, Sammy gave the operator the station to station number he wanted to call in South Carolina. After the fifth ring, a voice with which Sammy was very familiar answered. It was a simple hello, to which Sammy replied, "You were right, they're homesick." "I knew it. Whatta'ya wanna' do about'it?" "Will that plane still fly?" "I'm sure it will; when?" "If you'll check'it out, I'll call back tomorrow." "Get yourself a cheap throw-away phone and Mr. Ruiz can also buy a hundred-minutes on it, then call back to my cell; at six tomorrow evening. Does Mr. Ruiz understand?" "He does."

When he returned to their booth, Lula Mae asked Sammy where he had been; and when he told her he had been on the phone, naturally she wanted to know "who to". He told her that he had called to ask if the plane could return, and take her and Rulene back home. Lula Mae's jaw dropped, and she said, "Sammy, we didn't ask you to do that." "I know y'all didn't, but neither of you can ever be satisfied if you don't go back." "But, Sammy, what about you?" "Baby, let's get both of you back, and I'll be working on how and when I can come back; I'm thinking about that, but I haven't had time to plan it yet, but I will—and y'all can count on that. I repeat: I will come back, and it won't be long, either." From the restaurant to their home was a silent ride; not a word was spoken.

The following morning, Sammy went to a cell-phone store and bought a phone and four 30-minute cards. Lula Mae and Rulene begged Sammy to go back with them, at the same time. He told them that he would go with them, but that it would take him two or three-weeks to plan his return, because he could not afford to ever be recognized in the United States again, because he would be eligible for the electric chair. Just the mention of the electric-chair was all it took to start tears flowing from Rulene and Lula Mae.

Sammy, as requested by his South Carolina contact, made his 6:00 p.m. call, as promised. Using his cell phone, Sammy got an answer on the first ring. He didn't waste time, and got right to the reason for his call. "Hello, as you suggested, I bought a cell phone and four thirty-minute cards this morning. And as far as the trip I mentioned yesterday—lets put that on hold for about three weeks; I need time to plan how I can live in that area. I'm considering letting word out that I died in a traffic accident, and that my body was cremated. What do you think of that idea?" "You might be on to something with that. I'll be thinking about that between now and the next time we talk. Is that all for now?" "Is my number displayed on your phone?" "Yes." "I'll keep it on around the clock; so long for now." "So long my friend."

CHAPTER THIRTY THREE

After sitting around their house for five days, and no ideas coming to mind, Sammy decided to take a walk around downtown Guadalupe to see if a change of scenery might help him become more creative. He had been walking for well over an hour when he noticed a bench in a lush, green park setting that covered an entire square-block.

While sitting there on a park bench, Sammy observed an ambulance passing, and then stopping for a red-light. Suddenly, while looking at that ambulance stopped at the red-light, a green-light came on in Sammy's head. He thought—that's it! That's it! If I set-up an ambulance service I would not only be able to make money with it; I would also be able to move from place to place in an ambulance! I could fake being an accident victim, a heart attack victim or most any illness, all of which would require facial cover in the form of an oxygen mask, bandages, and etcetera. Sammy jumped up off the park bench and headed for home with new enthusiasm.

Lula Mae saw Sammy rushing across the yard and she met him at the front-door, "Sammy, what in the world is wrong?!" "Baby, there ain't nuthin' wrong; but everything's right!" Then Sammy went on to explain why he was so excited; and Lula Mae and Rulene also thought the ambulance company was a great idea; and they wanted to know when he was going to get started on setting it up. He told them that he was glad they liked the idea, but to try to settle down so they could be rational, and possibly contribute some good ideas.

Sammy was eager to call his friend in South Carolina, but he wouldn't mention any details without their conversation being pay-phone to pay-phone; so he got in the Ford Explorer and drove forty-seven miles to the opposite side of the city of San Jose, where he found a pay-phone in a fairly secluded location. When his friend in South Carolina answered his home phone, Sammy asked him to write down the pay-phone from which Sammy was calling, and then to go to a pay-phone and call him back. He told Sammy that it would take him about fifteen minutes to get to a pay-phone.

It was twenty-minutes before Sammy's pay-phone rang, and when it did, he literally snatched the receiver from the phone's hanger; and got right to the point—telling his South Carolina friend the basic advantages of his perceived new-business plan. His friend was very enthusiastic about what Sammy told him; even asking when the plane should come to get them. Sammy told him that he had not had time to think that far-out; but he left no doubt that they were anxious to get back home. He told his friend that they were living in a very nice place, but that there was only one United States of America; and, "we're anxious to cautiously return there".

When the Paul's were sitting at the supper table that evening, Sammy told Lula Mae and Rulene that there was another matter they needed to discuss, and that although they would not find it to be a pleasant subject, it had to be talked about. The two women looked at each other but didn't say anything; then, all of a sudden, Lula Mae said, "Well for goodness sake, Sammy, what is it?" Finally, Sammy spoke, "We'll have to fake my death." "What?!" Lula Mae literally yelled it out. "Yes, you'll have to pretend I was killed in an automobile accident, or something; and then you'll need to have my body cremated, supposedly, of course; and I had requested that there not be a service conducted for me; that all I wanted done was for the two of you to scatter my ashes on a beach that we had visited down on the Pacific Coast of Costa Rica.

When Sammy had his business-plan clearly in his head, he again went over it with Lula Mae and Rulene: “We’ll find a suitable building near Interstate-26, on the northwest side of Columbia, somewhere between Bush River Road and Broad River Road exits. Being right-in close to the exit from the Interstate is a must. We can use a closed-down service station building with four or five bays, in which to house the ambulances. The service station office can be made suit. Finding something suitable should not be too difficult. The two of you will have to be the faces of the business. I can assist y’all with the big decisions, but the hour to hour operational decisions will be yours. You’ll need to have good drivers who know the area. You can start-off with just one unit; no need to try to be the biggest in the area; just grow into the business; it’s not as if we’re depending on the business for a living; just remember what’s in that Swiss Bank Account.

When I need to go somewhere, I’ll go as the patient, and if we need to stop for some reason, I’ll be lying back there with a big-ole oxygen mask on. We’ll also need some fake bandages; ones that can quickly be installed over my face.

CHAPTER THIRTY FOUR

Five days later, Reid Garrison and his copilot arrived at Juan Santamaria International Airport in the city of San Jose, in the San Jose Province of Costa Rica. Reid taxied to a vacant building about three-hundred feet farther down the runway from Moreno-Cruz Aircraft Services. Again, Reid went in under false aircraft I.D. numbers, but not the same ones as before. Sammy pulled the white Ford Explorer close-up beside the Gulfstream to expedite transfer of their personal possessions. Sammy then returned the Ford to the parking area in which he found it, and as he had been instructed to do, he would toss the key when back in South Carolina. The car rental company would have duplicates.

Reid Garrison's total time on the tarmac this trip was nine-minutes. Reid was lucky. He was given clearance for take-off directly ahead of a Delta Boeing-747, and as on his previous trip there, Reid was able to begin his takeoff roll without first coming to a stop. He had decided to land for refueling at the same out-of-the-way airport that he had patronized on his first trip to Costa Rica. After his second takeoff in less than forty-five minutes, Reid's copilot filed a flight plan to Athens Municipal Airport, Athens, Georgia. Reid had no intention of flying direct to Athens. First, he would deliver his three passengers to the Greenwood County Airport, Greenwood, SC; after which would come the final leg of his flight; the seventy-miles from Greenwood to Athens.

At 11:17 p.m., Reid Garrison greased the wheels of the Gulfstream-450 onto the Greenwood County Airport runway; returning Lula Mae, Rulene and Sammy Paul to their native South Carolina. Sammy waved for Mott Gaines, his father-in-law, to drive out onto the tarmac, up close to the Gulfstream. Mott and

Daisy Gaines and the Paul's greeted each other as if they had been apart for many years, when in reality, their separation had been for only ten-weeks and three-days; however, the Gaines and Paul families, until two-weeks earlier, had lived a few-days over two months with the fear that they might never again lay eyes on each other, and just the thought of that possibility was enough to cause the women to cry tears of joy as they deplaned at the Greenwood County Airport.

Daisy staked-out the center of the back seat, saying, "I'm gonna' have my girls on both sides'a me, and I'm gonna' hold onto'em from now on; I might never let'em outta' my sight again—as long as I live." And after saying that, Daisy, Lula Mae and Rulene started crying again and did so, off and on, all the way home to Silverstreet; but now, their tears were tears of joy.

CHAPTER THIRTY FIVE

After Sammy Paul returned to South Carolina from Costa Rica, he was constantly aware of the fact that he absolutely must stay out of sight; unable to go out into the public domain ever again, he was constantly telling himself, "always be on guard, never stand in front of a window, or an open door, or any other place that I might be seen." And anytime he wanted to, or needed to go somewhere, he must do so in the back of an ambulance; always posing as the sick or the injured, thus the bottom line: Sammy was, realistically, a prisoner among the free; but even that circumstance, he reasoned, was immeasurably better than being locked in a cell, or lying dead in a box six feet below the grass. After having killed 331 people at the death-row facility, and the two punks who raped and murdered his and Lula Mae's daughter, Ruth Charlene Paul, Sammy was fully aware that he had reserved 333 tickets to the Electric Chair.

According to an obituary that appeared in the Newberry and Columbia newspapers, Sammy Paul had died as the result of a fall from the roof of his residence in Costa Rica, and as stipulated in his will, he was cremated, and his ashes scattered on a beach in Costa Rica. But naturally, the report of his death was not believed by all the people who read the newspaper reports, however, it was believed that the hunt for Sammy, after the reports, was much less intense than it would have otherwise been. The public reasoning seemed to be, "who the hell wants to be out there looking for a man who reportedly was killed in a fall from his rooftop, was then cremated, and his ashes scattered on a beach in Costa Rica? Not me."

Sammy's close friend, Warden Curt Galloway, the one he had been talking with on the phone shortly before his family's return to South Carolina, called him one day about eight-weeks after his return home, and told him that The Justice Seekers would like to meet with him. Sammy was surprised, and his first thought was that he should tell them "no thank you", but after thinking it through objectively, including the fact that it was from The Justice Seekers that his family's million-dollars came, he agreed to the meeting.

His friend told him that one of the The Justice Seekers owned a house on Lake Murray, and that's where the meeting would be held. At the appointed time, and at the identified road address; 6969 Foxfire Road, Lula Mae and Rulene delivered Sammy to the meeting in their recently acquired first ambulance; in which they would sit and eat their pizza while watching their nine-inch portable television, and waiting for Sammy's meeting to end.

When Sammy arrived, The Justice Seekers were all there, and in the following order, they lined-up to meet Sammy and shake his hand: Martha P. King of Lancaster, SC; Emmett F. Cox of Charleston, SC; Annabelle M. Killingsworth of Athens, GA; Wade Hampton Montgomery of Columbia, SC; Austin Lawrence Thomas of Greenville, SC; and then came the shocker for Sammy; the last member of the Justice Seekers was Curtis George "Frogman" Galloway of Marion, SC, Sammy's former warden at the 'big-house'. It was mutually agreed, between Curt and Sammy, that the best friend they ever had was each other. It would have been impossible to measure the respect they had for each other, and the confidence they had in each other. Curt and Sammy admitted, to the other five members of The Justice Seekers, that their love for each other was equal to that which only brothers would normally feel.

Sammy had assumed that Curt Galloway was a message carrier for The Justice Seekers; but it had never crossed his mind that Curt was one of the 'Big-Dogs'. Following dinner, each of the members congratulated and thanked Sammy for the good deed he had done at the Capital Punishment Center during the mock-execution.

Sammy's willingness to figure-out how to electrify every jail-cell-bar in the Capital Punishment Center and to then personally push the lever that sent twenty-three thousand volts of electricity surging through the entire jail-cell system had forever endeared him to The Justice Seekers. For years they had been trying to figure-out how to deliver justice in a place where justice nearly always proved to be dead. And then one day, while Warden Galloway and Sammy were in the warden's office enjoying an "old-fashion noon dinner", compliments of Daisy Gaines, Sammy's mother-in-law, the warden mentioned that in his opinion, "the entire death-row crowd should be electrocuted without delay", and right-then Sammy's fertile-mind started working on the solution that was destined to finally deliver justice; by delivering to the sixty-three murderers of men, women and children, precisely what the trial judges had ordered years earlier; up to twenty-nine years earlier in one case! Can you just imagine twenty-nine years of appeals? Just how in the name of hell can twenty-nine years of appeals be justified?

Sammy Paul personally delivered the verdict of The Justice Seekers: "All Appeals Denied".

Sammy not only carried-out the sentences that had been imposed by judges up to twenty-nine years earlier; he also eliminated twenty-three death-penalty opponents from the South Carolina State Legislature; and seventeen representatives from the non-capital punishment states in the U.S. And now, get this: less than thirty-minutes before the mock-execution march began; into the facility ran a last death-penalty opponent who entered a cell exactly seven-minutes before march-time, and if he had not been a VIP, the supervisor of admissions would not have allowed the entry of South Carolina's Democrat Governor Timothy Lackey.

The last two-hundred twenty-seven death penalty opponents were from countries scattered all over the World. Most of them were the much-cursed towel-heads. The mass-electrocution sent a loud, clear message to foreigners all over the world: Do not try to impose your will on the United States, especially not South Carolina, but if you do—just look at what could happen to you. All Appeals Denied.

Sammy thanked the six members for what they had done for him, after which, he told the members what he, Lula Mae and Rulene had been doing since the big event at the Capital Punishment Center. In a little side-bar meeting, Wade Montgomery, Chief Justice of the South Carolina State Supreme Court, impressed upon Sammy the importance of keeping private the names of each and every one of the Justice Seekers; and that included keeping it from his family, too. He also assured Sammy that his still being alive would also be kept secret by The Justice Seekers. Sammy told Justice Montgomery, "Don't worry; no-one, at no-time, will ever get me to say that what happened that night at the capital punishment center was ordered by The Justice Seekers. I would die to keep from telling that." Justice Montgomery, with his left hand around Sammy's upper-arm, said, "Sammy, Warden Galloway long ago convinced the other five of us Justice Seekers that you're "rock-solid", and that's good enough for us. I wish for you and your family the very best, Sammy."

Lula Mae and Rulene, referring to themselves as "women entrepreneurs", worked hard and forged ahead with "Safe Ride Ambulance Service", while Sammy and his close friend, Curt Galloway, worked behind the scenes to help build what, after only a year in business, was already turning a very decent profit; but even more important than the profit was the fact that it also enabled Sammy to get out and about, whereas, if he had been forced to hide indoors every-minute of every-day, he most likely would have gone crazy.

CHAPTER THIRTY SIX

In the spring of 2010, after Sammy, Lula Mae and Rulene had returned from Costa Rica, he had been fortunate to enjoy almost fifteen years of freedom in the place he wanted to be; which was with his wife, his daughter and his mother-in-law and father-in-law, Daisy and Mott Gaines.

Sammy gave himself an occasional pat on the back for thinking of starting the ambulance service that gave him the freedom he had enjoyed for the past fourteen-plus years; even though it was not total-freedom, it sure beat being locked in a jail-cell deep in the bowels of 'The Big House", the biggest, baddest prison in the entire system of the South Carolina Department of Corrections.

On August 21, 2011, Safe Ride Ambulance Service received a call requesting an ambulance to transport a comatose patient from the Newberry Clinic to the Medical University of South Carolina in downtown Charleston, a hundred-forty-eight mile drive each way. Rulene and her mother, Lula Mae, decided to make the trip and suggested to Sammy that he ride along; after all, the patient was comatose and in that condition wouldn't even know that he, himself, was in an ambulance. After picking-up the patient at the clinic, they went home to get Sammy. Two hours and twenty minutes later they were removing the patient from the ambulance at the medical center in Charleston.

As soon as the patient was removed from the ambulance, Sammy replaced him on the gurney for the hundred-forty-eight mile ride back up Interstate-26 to Newberry.

Rulene was driving the ambulance in the right-hand lane with her right-turn signal on, preparing to go from I-26 onto Hwy-219 by taking the ramp at Exit-76, just two-miles southeast of Newberry. There was a light-green Chevrolet 4-door sedan immediately in front of the ambulance, and it, too, was flashing right turn. The Chevy had passed the ambulance about five-minutes earlier, and from her elevated position, Rulene had looked right down into the green Chevy being driven by a thirty-fivish woman, with a boy about ten in the front and two younger girls in the back seat.

Rulene looked in her rearview mirror and saw two cars approaching in the left lane at break-neck speed: a red Corvette in front with a state trooper, with all lights flashing, right on the Corvette's bumper. The green 4-door Chevy had just begun to start up the exit-ramp when the Corvette and the trooper's car passed the ambulance running wide-open, and all of a sudden the Corvette, without warning, cut across in front of the Chevy—which had already started up the ramp, and nothing less than a miracle prevented the Corvette from plowing into the Chevy, and it so frightened the woman driver that she over-reacted, and while attempting to slam on the brakes, she missed the brake pedal and stomped the accelerator to the floor instead; and then, in an attempt to miss the three-legged tower that supported four high-voltage power-lines, she turned the steering-wheel sharply to the left and turned the car over; and on it's mid-air roll, the car's roof slammed into a leg of the tower and bent the leg severely enough to cause the tower to lean about thirty-degrees, far enough to break two of the four high-voltage lines.

The green Chevrolet came to rest with its roof against the tower, the right side on the ground, the left side facing skyward and with the bottom facing Interstate-26. Rulene had pulled over onto the shoulder of the road, and while she and Lula Mae sat there in a state of shock, Sammy opened the back door of the ambulance, and without hesitating to consider that he might be recognized by the state trooper, he jumped out and started running toward the Chevrolet while calling back over his shoulder to Lula Mae and Rulene to call the Sheriff's office and tell'em what happened, and to get two or three ambulances out there on the double, and for the two of them to, "stay inside our ambulance".

The trooper who had been chasing the Corvette had turned around under the bridge over the Interstate, came back, parked in the median and started running toward the Chevrolet with a fire extinguisher in his hands. He had seen the flicker of flames coming from under the hood of the car. Sammy told the trooper that he should stay back closer to the highway, that he, Sammy, had seen two of the high-voltage lines break and fall to the ground, and that if the tower leaned over any more the remaining two lines might also come down. Hearing that high-voltage power lines were on the ground, with two more possibly coming down any second; the trooper, who didn't need any more convincing, back-pedaled and let Sammy bring the woman and children out to him.

Sammy, moving rapidly, climbed up on the left front door, unlocked it from the inside, while silently thankful that the left-front window was rolled down, reached into the back seat and unlocked the door and opened it from the outside. Noticing that both of the girls were still strapped in their seatbelts, Sammy softly whispered more thanks while unfastening the girl's seatbelt, and then lifting her out and placing her on the grass about forty feet behind the car; then, still moving quickly, Sammy climbed back up on the car and let himself down far enough to unbuckle and lift the second girl out and place her beside the one that lay crying on the grass; and they wrapped their arms around each other and asked where their mother and brother were, and when Sammy told them they were still in the car and that he was going back for them right then, they both started calling for "mother and Freddie".

Sammy was working as though he was a programmed, smooth-running machine as he again pulled himself back up on the car and opened the door. He quickly realized that lifting the mother out of the car was not going to be easy. Luckily, she had the armrest pulled down between her and the boy, and when he unbuckled her, she was partially held in place by the armrest. Using his long, strong arms and big hands to full advantage, Sammy wrapped his left arm around her waist, while holding himself up out of the car by locking his right-arm around the post between the front and back doors, he simply used his God-given brute-strength to hoist the unconscious woman up and out of the car; and then he carried her over and placed her between her daughters who immediately started kissing her and telling her how much they loved her—and urging her to "please wake-up". When Sammy got back up on the side of the car, the boy, Freddie, as the sisters had called him, came-to. He was able to unbuckle himself and stand so Sammy could lift him out of the car. The trooper called for Sammy to hurry, that the fire under the hood was gaining momentum.

Just as Sammy ran back to get the fire extinguisher that the trooper had brought, he heard someone yell, "Get out from there, Sammy, that car might explode!" Sammy knew the voice he heard was that of Sheriff Bo Chrisley, and as Sammy moved away from the car, it did explode, shaking the leaning-tower against which the car was resting; and as Sammy looked upward, the third cable to break whip-lashed toward Sammy and wrapped three times around him. Sammy quivered, convulsed, and still shaking, fell to the ground. The tower moved again, causing the power-line that wrapped around him to jerk free and away from Sammy far enough for Sheriff Chrisley to scurry up to where he was lying to try to find a pulse. There was none.

Lula Mae and Rulene didn't see Sammy get electrocuted, but when they looked up that way and saw him on the ground, they jumped out of the ambulance and went to him as fast as they could, but Sheriff Chrisley had spread a blanket over him before they got there. The sheriff took Lula Mae and Rulene aside and assured them that Sammy was gone, and that nothing could be done for him. He asked if Sammy had a living will, and when told that he did, he asked if it stipulated what was to be done with his body. Lula Mae and Rulene, were so grief stricken they were barely able to talk, but Lula Mae did manage to tell Sheriff Chrisley that Sammy was to be cremated, and his ashes buried in the plot with Charlene, their deceased daughter.

Sheriff Chrisley very gently reminded Lula Mae and Rulene that since they had reported to the authorities in South Carolina that Sammy had died in an accident in Costa Rica and his ashes scattered on a beach down there, he would strongly recommend that Sammy be taken to the funeral home in Greenwood, the one with a crematorium, and have him cremated him that night. Both women agreed, and Sheriff Chrisley told them that he would wrap Sammy in the blanket he had spread over him and get a couple of his deputies to help him place his body in their ambulance, and then he would personally drive them to the crematorium in Greenwood. He suggested that the two of them might want to ride in the back of the ambulance with Sammy. That pleased them, and the sheriff had a couple of his deputies help him place Sammy on the gurney in the back of their ambulance. Sheriff Chrisley, and two of his deputies, gently placed Sammy in the ambulance, and then seated Lula Mae on one side of him and Rulene on the other side for the forty-one mile ride to Greenwood.

Sammy's ashes were buried in a stainless steel water-tight canister in the soil above Charlene's vault and as directed in Sammy's will and in Lula Mae's will, when she passed, she would be cremated, and the canister containing Sammy's ashes would be extracted from the soil above Charlene's vault, and then Lula Mae's ashes would be mixed with Sammy's. The canister would be taken to a welding shop, where the cap would be screwed on and then welded where it would be air-tight and water-tight. After that, Sammy and Lula Mae way would be together forever.

Sammy had added a codicil to his will—directing that when he died, his dear friend, Curtis George "Frogman" Galloway was to be immediately notified; he was, and then Curt called each of the other five members of "The Justice Seekers" to deliver the news. Sammy's funeral was private, by invitation only, and included, in addition to the family: their minister, Sheriff Bo Chrisley, Curt "Frogman" Galloway and the other five anonymous members of The Justice Seekers. Every one of the invited guests attended the brief service.

Sammy Paul, a good man, had been driven to do things he never would have considered doing if those two lousy, rotten thugs had not raped and killed his and Lula Mae's precious daughter, Ruth Charlene Paul. That pushed him over the edge, and he decided that he "just had to do what he did to them, or he would have forever felt that he had let their daughter down". He was driven to kill those punks who took Charlene's life; for which Sheriff Chrisley, Sheriff Doolittle, Warden Galloway and many others, in and out of law enforcement, felt that he should not have had to serve even one day in confinement. And he sure as hell should not have been given a life sentence for what he did to those two sorry jerks.

Lula Mae Gaines-Paul, who some said grieved herself to death over losing Sammy, died on December 8, 2011, in the same bed she had shared with Sammy for fifty-seven years. She was 77. She, like Sammy, had instructed that she be cremated and that her ashes be buried in the same water-tight, stainless steel canister with Sammy's ashes. Her funeral, like Sammy's, was private.

Rulene, in 2001, married a man named Danny Adams, whom she had hired as an EMT (Emergency Medical Technician) and driver at “Safe Ride Ambulance Service”. They have a son, Sammy Mott Adams, 8, and a daughter, Lula Charlene Adams, 6. They make their home in the same house in which Lula Mae was raised, and where her Momma died.

Mott and Daisy Gaines, Lula Mae Gaines-Paul’s parents, died peacefully in 1997 and 1998 respectively.

The parents and grandparents were laid to rest in the same plot in which Ruth Charlene Paul, daughter of Sammy and Lula Mae was buried in 1976.

Curtis George “Frogman” Galloway, 86, was a World War II hero, and an All-America Tight-End at The University of South Carolina in 1949. Curt still enjoys life surrounded by his extensive family, and he resides in his boyhood home in Marion County, South Carolina, midway between Marion and Mullins; and he can be found there almost every day—with the exception of the four-weeks of every year he spends in the luxurious beach-front house on Hilton Head Island, SC, courtesy of the state of South Carolina. Curt is still robust, works-out every day, and even at his age, looks as though he could give a good account of himself in a fight. All bad-guys are forewarned: Don’t mess with “Frogman” Galloway; because he still knows how to win.

FROM THE AUTHOR

Dear Readers:

Many thanks to you for reading "All Appeals Denied"; I sincerely hope you enjoyed the story, and if you're so inclined, I will appreciate your recommending it to your friends.

Have you read "Deadly Revenge", published in October 2010? It is available through: Amazon.com, Barnes & Noble, and other book-sellers. It is also available through me, James Knox, by calling my Verizon cell number: 864-313-0836.

My third book, "Justice Southern Style", should be ready by late June 2012.

I appreciate your patronage, and I look forward to hearing from you.

Respectfully,

James Knox
www.murder-crime-romance-jknox.com